The Search

A Novel

Gordon Duncan

PROLOGUE

Seven hundred years ago, the lights of western civilization flickered. Political and natural disasters ravaged the lands to the north in Europe and east toward Egypt. In northern Africa, steps were taken to protect the king's wealth from the struggles expected ahead.

It was cold beyond anything the men had ever experienced or heard about. The animal skins they had been given to wear earlier that day were appreciated but not enough against the cold, wind, and snow. The barefoot teams of two struggled to carry their loads in the high altitude and thin air but were pressed to finish the day's job while there was still daylight, after which weather conditions would only worsen.

Carefully, they positioned their loads in the exact positions they were instructed to do by these new and strange masters. That being done, they were led through a small gap in the rocks that opened into a huge cavern. Food, drink, warmth, and a small piece of gold for the day's work were given to all, along with a silent death, miles in the sky.

NORTHEAST
MASSACHUSETTS
CITIES AND TOWNS

Amesbury
Salisbury
Merrimac
West
Newbury
New
buryport
Haverhill
Newbury
Methuen
Groveland
Georgetown
Rowley
Lawrence
North
Andover
Boxford
Ipswich
Andover
Rockport
Topsfield
Hamilton
Essex
Tewksbury
Middleton
Wenham
Gloucester
Wilmington
North
Reading
Danvers
Beverly
Billerica
Lynnfield
Reading
Peabody
Manchester-
by-the-Sea
Burlington
Wakefield
Salem
Bedford
Woburn
Stoneham
Saugus
Lynn
Melrose
Marblehead
Winchester
Swampscott
Lexington
Arlington
Medford
Malden
NAHANT
Lincoln
Belmont
SOMERVILLE
Everett
Revere
Waltham
Watertown
CAMBRIDGE
Chelsea
Winthrop
Weston
Newton
Brookline
Wellesley
BOSTON
Needham
Hull
Dover
Dedham
Milton
Quincy
Westwood
Cohasset
Medfield
Weymouth
Hingham
Scituate
Norwood
Briantree
Canton
Randolph

ONE

In the Beginning

What a beautiful spring morning, thought Joe, with a slight smile of satisfaction on his face. He paused and looked around for a few seconds before stepping out from his Cambridge apartment into the cool March air. For the first time in the twenty years since finishing college, Joe wouldn't be an employee of the United States government. Today, he began a new life with a new job in a new city.

Wish me luck, he thought before backing his car from its parking spot. Looking about on his drive along the Charles River, he couldn't help but think how Cambridge had...

"More spies per capita than any other city in the world, including Washington D.C., people. This shouldn't come as a surprise to anyone, with Harvard, MIT, and who knows how many dozens of universities and hundreds of R&D firms operating in and about the city."

Just twenty minutes later, the mood of the day had changed dramatically as Walter Simpson barked his introductory speech to his new project management team at Cambridge Metals Laboratory, or CML for short.

Walter had met with each team member individually during the interview process. This was the first meeting as a team. He paced side to side in the front of their conference room as he spoke with a pained and intense expression on his face, waving his right arm in emphasis.

"Do not underestimate a spy's tenacity, patience, or creativity in getting what they want. These spies will probe for your weaknesses and take whatever time is required to find them. Given the nature of our new project, secrecy will be of the utmost importance. Only people with a Secret security clearance from the Department of Defense (DOD) are allowed to work on this project, which has been given the code name 'Pokey.' The same words of caution are true with others you may interact with at other locations or agencies. Be careful!" He then paused and turned to the side to speak with a messenger who had interrupted and requested his immediate attention on something.

The reasons for secrecy were obvious. The United States military has been involved in training and counter-terrorism activities in Africa for decades. The war on terror has escalated this involvement to the point where there were now an estimated seven thousand U.S. military and civilians in northern Africa in addition to an estimated 50,000 in the Middle East.

Most of these outposts are for training purposes; however, some are for special operations activities, with multiple drone bases used to gather intelligence and on occasion, get directly involved in a military action. Casualties have been suffered throughout the region. Several grisly setbacks may have been avoided if there had been prompt warning of an imminent ambush.

With the U.S. Congress and the general public upset at the sacrifices being made by some of our country's "best and brightest" in the defense of liberty and human rights, accelerated action was taken by our advanced intelligence and military weapons teams to make quantum leaps in drone development and weaponization.

The official goal of the project was to determine how much faster image recognition, identification, and analysis would improve our military's ability to respond appropriately to enemy movements. The primary use of this technology would be in drones flying in and satellites flying over the current and anticipated future zones of aggression which focused on the hilly and usually barren terrains of North Africa and the Middle East.

After several minutes, Walter turned and readdressed the team, "My apologies for the interruption. Again, my name is Walter Simpson, but going forward, please call me Skip. I'm the project manager and will be your boss for at least the next two years on this very special effort. My boss is the program director, Mr. Jones. Mr. Jones is purely an administrative contact with Washington. You'll have no reason to ever contact him directly. Please direct everything through me. Is that clear? Please make sure your staffs understand this as well.

"I run a structured ship. Our work week starts precisely

at eight thirty in the morning Monday through Friday with forty-five minutes for lunch and the workday ends precisely at five fifteen p.m. We're a paper mill, people. Weekly reports will be expected to be submitted on time every Friday afternoon, and they need to be thorough. We will have project review meetings once a month. This stage of the program is funded for two years, which means we must plan on wrapping things up in eighteen months to allow for six months of writing, corrections, clarifications, and creating a request for more time and money!

"As leaders, it's important that we know a little something about each other. Let's go around the room and introduce ourselves. I'll start. I'm Skip, and I have over twenty years of experience with Department of Defense projects in the Greater Boston area. Prior to that, I was in the U.S. Air Force for a long time. I'm divorced with two expensive teenagers and live outside the city. Okay, that's me. Let's go!" One by one, the staff members stood up to introduce themselves. Joe started.

"Hello everyone, my name is Joe Logan. I'm forty-two, single, and live in Cambridge. I graduated from Dartmouth with a BSME and then went into the military and government work. I'm an ex-Army Ranger with some additional training and have spent a lot of time living and working in the Middle East and northern Africa. I'm a consultant now and eating on a regular basis.

"I'm on the team because of my background in geology, topography, and on-ground experience in the area where this project is expected to be put into service. I look forward to working with everyone."

"Good morning, my name is Sanjib Patel. I am thirty-two years old, a native of India but a naturalized United States citizen, and an expert in computer software. I am a graduate of Purdue with a BSEE and MSEE in computer science. I've worked in the Boston area for about eight years on previous DOD projects where I've managed large teams of engineers and successfully handled extremely complex problems and challenges. I am married, have two kids, and own a home in Medford."

"Hi, my name is Kevin Chen. I'm thirty, went to CalTech, and am a specialist in computer hardware. I too have BSEE and MSEE degrees. I'm American citizen, born in California, single, and live in Somerville. I've worked in the area for five years and also look forward to working with the team."

"Good morning, everyone, my name is Mildred Cronin, and I oversee HR activities. I'll work closely with you as we have a lot of hiring and training to do. I live locally with my husband and three cats."

"Good morning, I'm the program finance manager, Bob O'Neill. I'll be trying to keep all of you in line. I have four grown children and live in the suburbs. I've worked for various companies in the Boston area for about forty years. Stay under budget. Nice to meet you."

Skip was a bit gruff from decades in or around the military. Standing about five foot ten inches tall with a full head of wavy hair and half of it still its original brown color, he was a type "A" personality. His speech pattern was staccato... rapid fire and abrupt. High blood pressure and cholesterol were good bets. Bob was over six feet tall and trim, with a relatively laid-back personality. While Skip and Bob wore contact lenses, Mildred stayed with glasses and could have passed as a schoolteacher or librarian.

The new blood, the team that would do the work, was in jeans and casual shirts, and wearing either running shoes or hiking boots. Sanjib had a bit of an arrogant swagger to him and a slight Indian accent. Kevin displayed Chinese stoicism (i.e. he was quiet), and being from California, no discernible accent. Joe came from upstate New York at a point north and west of the strong dialects of New York City and Boston. Joe, too, had no discernible accent.

Sanjib used both hands when describing himself while Kevin stood, said his peace, and sat, returning to his obnoxious (to some) habit of twirling a pen in his hand. You couldn't tell anything by their clothing or hairstyle. Kevin was the taller of the two at five foot eleven, versus Sanjib's five foot eight and Joe's six foot one heights. All were slim, well-groomed, and without glasses. Sanjib had a moustache, and Joe a light beard.

"Are there any questions?" asked Skip.

Kevin raised his hand and asked, "Where are our offices?"

"Down the hall to the left. They are all about the same size and were assigned alphabetically, so don't get upset if your office isn't to your liking. Your name should be written on a piece of cardboard and taped to the door. They are being cleaned up this week. Your teams will use two large shared offices at the end of the building. The lab is being set up across the hall. My office is just to the right. You'll need to help in the lab as required to ensure things are installed correctly. Anyone else?"

Sanjib slowly raised his hand and with false curiosity and modesty asked, "Sir, the project name is Pokey. Is that like the (pause) hokey pokey?"

Skip was a little agitated by the question. "It's Pokey, like slow poke. Higher-ups decided to avoid any name which could imply speed. Are there any more questions? If not, that's it for today. I'll see you all bright eyed and bushy tailed tomorrow morning on time. Go ahead and get familiar with the facility. You'll find a lunchroom down the hall, capable of serving nothing. You'll need to bring your own or go out for lunch. Remember, it is forty-five minutes. Joe, please stay for an extra minute. Everyone else, have a good day."

After everyone had filed out of the conference room, Skip stared at Joe quite seriously. "That was a very brief summary you gave for twenty years of 'experience.' What neither of us said today was that you have top-secret clearances from the National Security Administration (NSA), and the DOD, and speak multiple regional languages. Who are you?"

Joe wasn't expecting this but, after a pregnant pause on his part, he replied, "I can't tell you much more about my past than I already have because it's classified. I did get to know the cultures, languages, terrains, etc. of much of the region. I lived and worked there for years. I'm here for the reasons you gave for the project's existence. I have the local and operational experience. I'm extra insurance. That's it."

Skip, after sizing Joe up for a few seconds, said, "Okay, go ahead and catch up with your teammates. See you tomorrow morning."

Joe could understand Skip's curiosity and suspicion. Odd and strange people had a habit of showing up on government projects. Some were of value, some looked for a free ride courtesy of powerful friends, and others were, of course, spies! He was surprised, however, that so much of his background may have been passed on to his future boss.

Joe's additional training wasn't something he ever intended to tell anyone about. It was far more intense than anything he experienced in college and required five years to complete, not four. While at Dartmouth, he not only excelled scholastically, but he also participated in crew and long-distance running. He was mentally and physically tough, and this was noted by important people in the college administration, who approached him about an unusual career with the government.

The additional training was over and above that given to U.S. Army Rangers, which was already quite rigorous. It was premised on having to survive on one's wits alone in the desolate hills that are much of northern Africa through Pakistan. The expectation was that in all but a few instances, Joe and others with similar training could be dropped from a plane or disappear from a local office and be picked up months later in good health, having been completely self-sufficient. Longer hair, a beard, and a need of a shower would be the only expected and noticeable differences.

Learning things like language, weapons use, religion,

clothing, local customs, and mannerisms were basic. Beyond that, it meant you needed to understand ancient methods of communicating in code, local geology, which animals could survive in what areas, and where could you find water and how could you purify it?

Joe knew how to make rescue signs out of whatever was available. Part of this was learning the qualities of various woods: how well did they burn, and which were dense enough that most animals couldn't chew through them? What bugs or fish or even stones would glow in the dark under the right circumstances? It was well known that the Ute Indians of North America would put quartz crystals in ceremonial rattles and shake them to get them glowing brightly (or in Joe's case, to use as a warning or rescue signal). There were also health issues to the training. He knew to put sugar on a wound to disinfect it and to chew the bark of certain trees to reduce a fever. He also knew how to quickly detect a poison.

There could be extended and locally visible assignments. Explaining the presence of an obvious outsider in these very tribal countries could be difficult. If they were ever caught or killed, the United States government, if asked, would either deny any relationship with or knowledge of them, or when necessary, claim that they were missionaries for a fringe religious group. That would usually be enough to satisfy the media and politicians.

Very few people graduated from this non-diploma school, but those who did became valuable "deep-deep-deep state" intellectual assets of the United States government.

THE LAB

The team familiarized themselves with the lab facilities and office space on this, day one. The lab was put in an obscure building one mile east of the MIT campus in East Cambridge, to avoid student interaction and curiosity. On paper, the name "Cambridge Metal Laboratories" was a laboratory for the testing of metal fatigue for the power utilities. It was boring stuff, expected to draw no attention from anyone. It was secretly owned by MIT as part of their long-standing relationship with the Department of Defense.

The government had adopted this approach locally many times before to avoid too much scrutiny or attention, most notably with the development of the atomic bomb and advanced radar systems during the Second World War. The lab was located off campus but close enough to quickly access the library and other facilities as required. Harvard was two miles further west.

The building was of typical early 1950s construction, buff-yellow brick with worn and chipped green linoleum square floors, fogged glass doors that rattled when closed, large and ugly steel frame windows, and blinds occasionally punctured with old, noisy, and underpowered air conditioning units. Marks in the linoleum floor indicated where the lunchroom once had vending machines, but that was many years ago. Now it will be home to a coffee pot and refrigerator, nothing more, nothing less. It was a single-story building with a large basement below.

The parking lot was gated and fenced in with a security fob required to get in or to leave. Faded "No Trespassing" signs were posted everywhere with warnings about radiation exposure or the presence of corrosive chemicals included in the message. A power substation was off in a far corner of the parking lot which was large enough to hold one hundred cars. The building had two loading docks and may have housed a postal or electric utility operation at one time. The building was so nondescript that it should never draw a second look from anyone.

Heavy-duty, standard-issue steel desks with even heavier-duty steel chairs, two metal file cabinets, a metal bookcase or two, and a clock were the standard issue for this, and every government office ever built.

This place was right out of a cheap 1950s science fiction movie, missing only a calendar on the wall and a "thing-a-ma-bob" that would swing ominously whenever an atomic bomb exploded, the sound barrier had been broken, or a monster from beneath the sea was tromping through the neighborhood looking for lunch. The team wasn't impressed at all.

The building was now being renovated and outfitted with advanced military-grade equipment from various suppliers. Several contracts had been previously awarded to computer chip and other suppliers to get going in advance of the Pokey project being awarded. Pokey will assemble and test the completed packages from these other vendors. After Pokey, the equipment would be packaged and moved for field testing. Of course, things were properly camouflaged to make it look like a benign academic testing facility. For the near term, the job of the team was to assist the technicians in the installation and basic testing of the equipment. After everything had been installed, commissioned, and signed off, they would begin the actual project tests.

As noon approached, Joe, Sanjib, and Kevin walked several hundred feet down and across the street to try out a neighborhood sandwich shop for lunch. Like everything else in this neighborhood, this shop had seen better days. It was best identified by a seasoned Coca Cola sign placed above the door and against a green backdrop. After placing their orders, they found a booth in the corner and sat down. Quickly, their sarcasm and sharp wit came into play.

Sanjib started, "Can you believe that guy? He's right out of the 1960s NASA program. White shirt and skinny black tie; can you still buy ties like that? 'Don't talk to my boss?' And naming the project 'Pokey?' Are you kidding me?" He then broke into a little finger dance, tapping the salt and pepper shakers on the table while softly singing the hokey pokey song you hear at nearly every wedding.

Joe looked at Sanjib and said, "Yup, he's a control freak. After your hokey pokey comment, he's going to loooove you."

With a deadpan expression on his face, Kevin chimed in, "Actually, I've been told the chicken dance and the hokey pokey are traditional Indian wedding songs that people love to dance to at every Hindu wedding, you know with all of those arms… You put your left arms in, you take your left arms out, you put your right arms in, and you shake them all about, you do the…"

Sanjib cut him off and replied tersely, "No, they are not, Buddha boy."

Kevin maintained his deadpan face and wagged his finger at Sanjib, "Now the challenge to all of us will be to avoid humming that stupid ditty during work hours or, even worse, when you're up front, making a presentation. Try keeping a straight face, bro."

Sanjib began to appreciate the challenge of this repartee, "I don't know about the two of you, but I have an image to keep up, and I can't do it if I keep thinking of myself as the pokey man. I guess Skip's right in that sense; no one is going to brag about or show any interest in a project called Pokey. You guys are single with your fancy cars and apartments and stuff. I can't imagine either of you trying to impress a chick with your job. 'Yeah, babe, stick with me cause I'm with (he paused and wagged his eyebrows) project Pokey.' Then with a leering look on his face, he said, 'Let me show you my Pokey, honey.' It won't work." After a quick look at his sandwich, he added, "This food isn't helping my self-esteem either. What is this stuff?"

They all started to eat their sandwiches, which were saved by French fries and pickles. After a minute or so, the conversations started again. Kevin had enough of the earlier topic and changed the subject, "What did you think about the spy lecture? They give one at the beginning of every new project. I haven't seen one so emotional before."

Joe jumped in, "Yeah, the spy lecture was a bit over the top. Others I've seen were low key and procedural. I think it's his 'blow and go' personality, so we had better learn to live with it."

Sanjib quickly countered, "They can't touch me, for I..." now putting a hand on his chest, "...am above reproach but..." and now looking at Kevin and speaking ever so slowly, "...they might tempt you with drugs, women, men, or comic books. Which do you think might work?"

Kevin, ignoring Sanjib, said, "I tell you what won't work is this food. I agree, it sucks. We can forget about coming back here. With only forty-five minutes for lunch, it looks like it's going to be a sandwich from home followed by real food and beer at dinner."

After a few more bites of food, Joe spoke again, "Hey, I know just the place for that beer, guys. Murphy's Pub. I've been there a few times. It's ten minutes from here and nice. I'll take you there tonight after work. The first beer is on me."

THE BARROOM

That first evening, Sanjib, Joe, and Kevin walked into Murphy's Pub in Somerville, located on a major boulevard with a lot of traffic. It was a typical old industrial New England corner bar and grill, two stories high, made of brick with ornate woodwork around the large windows facing the street. The woodwork was painted dark green; the ceiling was stamped tin sheet with the occasional slow speed fan for appearances. Air conditioning took care of everything now. It was a small market at one time, an A&P or a First National, with the large windows to display cans of soup or boxes of detergent in decades past.

There were some paved parking spots on the side of the building where another building may have been torn down and more parking in the back on a dirt lot. On a busy night, many people must find on-street parking in what is already a congested neighborhood. Joe stopped them as they entered the door and asked, "Hey, isn't this how a bunch of jokes begin… a Scotsman, an Indian, and a Chinaman walk into a bar and…" They gave him a shove and in they went.

This bar had become quite a successful watering hole for the many professionals who had transformed Somerville from a struggling blue-collar city of "three decker's" housing the city's factory workers to an upscale, expensive, and thriving city. Being two miles north of Boston and adjacent to Cambridge certainly helped. The once likely market had been transformed into a lively bar/tavern, serving food as well as having several different forms of entertainment over the course of the week.

In one corner, there was a small dance floor and a stage behind it for a band or other kinds of activities. Once a week, they had a trivia contest and another night was reserved for karaoke. As it turned out, it was trivia night with a first-place prize of one hundred dollars. After buying the second round of drinks for his two friends, Sanjib looked around the bar and suddenly shouted, "Holy shit, it's one of those guys!"

"What are you talking about?" asked Joe.

"I can't believe one of those little bastards came all the way here to Boston. Honest to Christ." Sanjib was obviously upset.

Now, Kevin was curious. "Really, Sanjib, what are you talking about?"

"My dad worked for an Indian steel company and had several overseas postings. When I was a small boy, and we were living in East Africa, my dad would often be asked to evaluate possible iron ore sites in the countryside. Sometimes, the rest of the family would join him. I remember these bastards in the Sudan, little pointy headed dudes with weird looks in their eyes. Somebody told them they were God's special children. There would be these festivals where these characters would dance and make weird noises.

"The 'tiger children,' they called them. They would bully my brother and me because we were foreigners, circling us and making these weird noises. It was scary for a little kid. I'm going to check this guy out and introduce myself." Sanjib went over and interrupted the conversation the man was having with someone. The tiger child was visibly surprised that a stranger just walked up to him in a bar and claimed to know who he was and where he was from.

Joe, meanwhile, looked around the bar at the various people, stopped, and slowly let out a "Wow, look-at-her!" Standing beside a table among a few older men in tweeds and ties was a gorgeous blonde. "My God, she is beautiful." He had good reason to feel this way. She was tall with plenty of curves and a money smile.

"Those guys she's with look like Harvard types," said Kevin. "It's odd for them to visit a bar in MIT territory. Perhaps they're conducting an urban study or something."

In the meantime, Sanjib had returned from his confrontation. He saw the trivia announcement and walked over to register for it. Returning to his workmates, he smugly announced, "Gentlemen, we need to stick around for the trivia contest. I'm really good at these things, and the one hundred bucks will pay for my bar bill."

"You mean our bar bill," said Joe.

"Nope, my bar bill," was the curt reply.

The trivia contest began one hour later after a little more alcohol had loosened up the crowd and quickly progressed from silly to quite serious. Fifteen people registered, most for fun but some for the recognition and prizes. What began with easy and funny questions like what color is an orange quickly progressed to more difficult and highbrow. This was to be expected given the crowd now full of college graduates with multiple degrees, trying to show off how smart they were. Thirty minutes later, it was down to two contestants, Sanjib and a short frizzy-haired woman who looked like she lived in the back of a library. The final question was presented by the game host to Sanjib to answer.

"Okay, sir, for the one hundred-dollar first place prize and a free beer: Who was the richest man to ever live?"

A pretentious and swaggering smile overtook Sanjib's face. He looked over the crowd and said loudly, "That's easy, John D. Rockefeller." He then pumped his fist in the air to signify victory, did a half turn, and walked back toward his friends at the bar.

"I'm sorry, that isn't correct," said the game host. This stopped Sanjib in his tracks. "Miss, do you know the correct answer?"

The frizzy-haired woman said meekly, "Is it Mansa Musa?"

"You're correct and are tonight's winner. Congratulations! How about a toast to our winner?" The crowd clapped and eagerly joined the host with the drink salute.

At this point, Sanjib wasn't a happy camper; his ego had been punctured. He turned and walked back to the game host and with a contorted expression on his face said, "I'm sorry, who did you say, Mickey Mouse? Mazda Miata? Isn't that a car?"

"All I can tell you, sir, is what's written on this card. It says he was the king of Mali seven hundred years ago and worth more than half a trillion dollars," was the host's polite and serious reply.

"What? I used to live in Africa; they don't have two pieces of cow shit to burn, eat, or trade. Half a trillion dollars; are you kidding me?" Sanjib was obviously embarrassed.

Joe and Kevin pulled Sanjib back to quiet him down while at the same time showing him no mercy.

"I thought you had played this game before," said Joe.

Kevin was next, "Did you really live in Africa or was it Atlanta? Even I knew it wasn't Rockefeller. Maybe you shouldn't drink before playing these games in a bar. Stay sober; next time, ask for water."

"Really, guys, would you've picked Rockefeller or mama mama mia from Mali?" replied a flustered Sanjib, trying to regain his composure. With all the commotion, no one noticed the Harvard crowd had left for the night.

MANSA MUSA'S WORLD

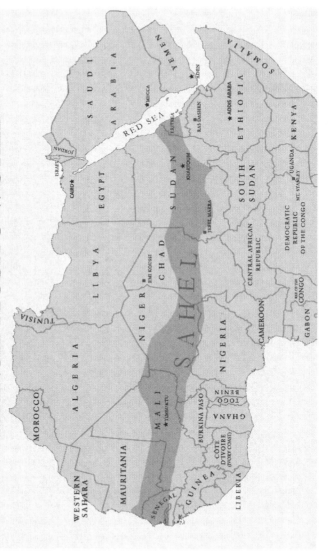

TWO

The Library

Joe frequently went to the MIT and Harvard libraries once the program got started to further investigate the terrain of Africa and the Middle East and to also read up on the latest developments in sensors and drones. These libraries are among the world's greatest. Together, they housed many millions of books, prints, maps, technical papers, etc. While he had worked and lived in the region before, the success of this project required a better understanding of the local geology. The soils were primarily sand, salt, and dust, the landscape varying shades of sandstone. In many ways, the sandstone areas looked like the American Painted Desert.

At one point in time, much of the Sahara desert was a sea and later a lake. Fossils in the rocks bore witness to that. Today's dust may have been muck at the bottom of a body of water thousands of years ago. Joe knew from his own experience that existing defense electronic equipment often had difficulties with signals being either absorbed or scattered by materials like this. Dust storms in this region were frequent and could last for as long as six days. They had been a substantial problem for military surveillance.

Joe was aware of the area under investigation, having spent a total of eleven years in the region, of which three years were in the Gulf, three years classified, and another five years on special assignment in northern Africa. He saw plenty firsthand, much of it not good. It ranged from the unique cultures, architecture, and cuisine, to the brutality of some regimes against Christians, Jews, and Muslims, to extreme poverty, extreme wealth, and in some cases, extreme kindness. Women were treated poorly, like or worse than animals or property. The women were beautiful though, and nice. The whole experience was burnt deeply into his memory and heart.

"Excuse me, but didn't I see you at Murphy's a few weeks ago?" interrupted a sweet and innocent-sounding female voice. My God, it was her, the blond goddess. Joe was sitting at a desk, and she was looking down at him with an armful of folders.

"Yes, I was there with some friends. You, too?" Incredibly, Joe said this with a straight face.

"Me, too! Hi, my name is Lexi," she said with a big smile and an outstretched hand. She must have been five foot eight, blue eyes, and incredibly clear skin. A white blouse matched with a gray pencil skirt accentuated the positives.

"My name is Joe. It's a pleasure to meet you." Her interest in him was understandable. Joe was a tall, handsome guy, with blue eyes, an athletic build, and a full head of brown hair with an occasional curl at the nape of his neck. He also had a beautiful skin tone, darker than you would expect of someone with primarily Northern European heritage, and indicative of either some "black Irish" or Mediterranean ancestry as well. He, too, had an engaging smile.

"Now I'm puzzled. Why would Harvard people with all of the nice places around here be all the way across town in a cheap bar in Somerville?"

"Well, we were attending a meeting nearby and stopped in for a drink. It was busy and seemed like a cool place. I could ask you the same question. Why were you there if you're studying at Harvard?"

"I actually work near MIT but have come here on occasion to research a few things on Africa. How about you? Are you a student?"

"I work here at Harvard in an African Antiquities section as an assistant to one of the directors. He needs research; I dig it out. Ancient cultures, languages, migrations. It's an interesting job."

Joe looked at her with a slight grin and a raised eyebrow and decided to flirt. "You have a slight accent; are you from Wistah?"

"No, silly, I'm not from Worcester. I moved here from the Ukraine ten years ago as a student and decided to stay."

"Oh, I see. Hmmm, you know it was an African question in the trivia contest at the bar that night that decided who won."

"That's right! I remember you and a Chinese guy had to calm an Indian fellow down. The poor guy thought he had won. Mansa Musa was the correct answer."

"Yep, he was upset. How do you know about this guy Mansa Musa?"

"Everyone in African studies knows about him. He's one of the mysteries of Africa. He was the king of Mali. Seven hundred years ago, he made a pilgrimage across Africa to Mecca. He took along fifty thousand people and two billion dollars in gold for gifts and to buy things. He gave away so much gold, he flooded the Middle East markets with it."

"Interesting stuff."

"Yes, but is it more than that? He didn't give all the gold away, yet he returned home with none. So where did it all go? Is it still out there hidden somewhere? Just a little bit of it is a lot of money. I could use it!" said Lexi with a soft voice and funny smile.

"Very interesting story. I wasn't aware of this guy. Maybe I can help you find it. I used to live and work in that area." Joe's flirting had moved from an attempt at humor to a serious approach.

"Really? What did you do?"

"Oh, it was government work, you know, farm aid and such. If I find anything about the good king and his gold, I'll let you know."

"That would be great, thanks. Well, I must go. It was nice talking with you. Maybe I will see you back here again," Lexi said as she turned, smiled, and waved goodbye.

Joe waved back and thought, *you can bet on it*. He also thought *Wistah... what an idiot*. Joe was too smitten by this encounter to question her encyclopedic recall of that evening at the bar.

DINNER AT SANJIB'S

The project had been moving along for several months with few unexpected issues. Although working for Skip certainly introduced an element of pressure and bluster, they were all adapting to it. The equipment was being successfully commissioned, and the team worked well together. So well, as a matter of fact, they socialized outside of work on a regular basis.

Sanjib invited some of his co-workers home for dinner one evening to celebrate with his family the East African holiday of Kachama. It was always held the first week of May. Sanjib's wife's name was Mah, and she too was of ethnic Indian descent but raised in East Africa. She was shy and tiny at five foot one inches tall. She was eight years Sanjib's junior at twenty-four years old. They had only been married for four years, arranged by their parents with their traditional wedding held back in India.

Sanjib had also invited his brother Ravi and his wife Nara. Ravi was in his early forties and had immigrated to the United States before Sanjib. He was your typical white shirt and gray slacks chemical engineer, sleeves usually rolled up and collar loosened for a cheap tie he purchased years and years ago. He was taller and heavier than Sanjib with a growing bald spot at the back of his head. With no children, his work was his life. Nara was in her early thirties and had a senior-level job within the human resources department at Harvard University.

She was attractive, demure, intelligent, of mixed Indian and East African blood, and more engaging than Mah. Both Mah and Nara were light skinned with fine facial features. Nara was much taller than Mah at five feet five inches and slender but still comfortably shorter than her husband. Both had beautiful black hair. While Mah's black hair hung long and braided, Nara's was short in a fashion favored by professionals.

Mah appeared to be deferential to her demanding husband. While Nara was certainly polite to her older and quiet husband and he to her, for some reason, she was distant. She was professionally polite and engaging but seemed to be the kind of person you couldn't get a read on, always guarding her true feelings. Her wardrobe would often appear out of place at a function that called for more relaxed attire. She was trying to fit in. She and Ravi were married locally in the Boston area two years ago, without parental intervention. Attending dinner that night from work were Kevin, Skip, and Joe.

Sanjib and Mah lived in the city of Medford, located about four miles north of the office. Medford was the home of Tufts University, known around the world primarily for its School of Diplomacy and School of Dentistry. In former years, it, like most of the cities and towns around Boston, was heavily into manufacturing. Like most of its peers in the area, Medford had morphed into a services and high-tech city, and its proximity to Boston and the area's cultural and recreational activities had seen the value of its homes skyrocket.

Sanjib and Mah were lucky to come across their three-bedroom six-room cape when they did. The five hundred thousand dollars they paid for this twelve-hundred-square-foot home was done with the couple fully knowledgeable of the substantial work and money that would be required to modernize it. It was a good deal in this hot housing market. Outside of the Northeast USA corridor or California, this pricing would make no sense at all, even after financial assistance from their families. It ate up a big chunk of their monthly income, but they were proud of their investment in their future.

Preparations had been finished, and Mah asked everyone to find a seat in their dining room to begin the festivities.

"So tonight, everyone, we're having traditional dishes from my home country of the Sudan. It's a mix of local and Indian recipes. I hope you like it," said Mah.

"I love it, and I'm sure Joe does, too, having lived there for a while?" questioned Sanjib.

"Is that right, Joe? Did you live in Khartoum?" asked Mah.

"No, I didn't live in Khartoum. I stayed there a few times and usually passed through to somewhere else."

"And where would that somewhere else be?" inquired a curious Nara. His hesitation in replying gave Sanjib an opening to clown around.

"Joe is too shy to say it, but he was a CIA assassin that roamed our part of the world bumping off people right and left. Guns, rocks, blow darts, poisonous snakes, under-cooked food; he used them all and was very good at what he did. If you're late returning a book to the library, pffft, a dart to the neck. Run a red light, a snake in your bed. Late on a payment, 'Here try this, it tastes really good!' On that basis, he was hired to work at CML."

"That's not true," said a serious Joe, shaking his head.

"No snakes? How about knives?"

Joe, now a little embarrassed, said, "I worked for several years in the area on behalf of the American government, farm aid and education. I can't go into any more details, or I'll have to kill you. I might do that anyway. I can say that the people generally were very humble and kind." He looked at Sanjib, smiling, signaling a slit across the throat.

"Well, aren't you intriguing!" said Mah with a half-smile and a little wag of her head. "Anyway, it took Nara and me awhile to find all the ingredients for this meal, but we got them. It's going to be an authentic East African dinner." She then placed the first course on the table.

Joe was excited and smiled. "Batumba beans! Wow, it has been a long time since I had these." He then smeared some on a piece of gurassa bread and took a big bite. Batumba beans are unique in that they are sweet and salty at the same time and oddly colorful. The colors turned many people off. Skip and Kevin followed suit, but not with the same enthusiasm or amount. Sanjib and Ravi dug right in. Course after course of unique and flavorful foods followed along with local drinks and Gala brand beer from Chad.

It was a pleasant evening full of great conversation and a lot of laughs. As he was leaving, Joe grasped Mah's hands, smiled, and looked her in the eyes and said, "Takume alkar farak bazum," to which she smiled. He then turned and said to everyone else, "Thank you for a very pleasant evening. I had a really good time."

Nara challenged him with, "Ezeek mau combit kolo."

His quick response, with a slight nod and a smile, was, "Ton kolo zamba. Good night everyone."

He then left with Skip and Kevin. They all drove their own cars home.

Mah turned to Sanjib, "Interesting fellow, Joe; who is he?"

"He's exactly what he said, ex-military familiar with the region on the program to help us with terrain recognition issues, yadi yada."

Nara quickly interjected herself into the conversation, pursing her lips and ever so slightly shaking her head, "There's more to it than that, Sanjib. His isn't a casual knowledge. He knew about Batumba beans, and they are local to the Dongola region up north, not Khartoum. He not only knew about them, but he knew they were good, a delicacy. Do you remember the first time I served them to you? You thought they were bugs, stripes and all! To the other guys, they could have been baked beans, striped baked beans, or bugs! He also thanked us in a local dialect in a very personal/familiar tense. This dinner meant something special to him, and he thanked Mah from his heart."

Sanjib turned to Mah and with a concerned look on his face, half kiddingly asked, "Was he hitting on you?"

Nara quickly answered him a little emphatically, "No, silly, but he was using words and a tense he must have used before in the Sudan with people he was familiar with. I'll take it further. Anyone, what does "Ezeek mau combit kolo" mean?"

"I'm not sure," said Mah. The others shook their heads.

"It's a Sudanese bush country local colloquialism meaning, 'We hope to be honored by your presence again.' He knew what I was saying and replied, 'I hope so too.'"

Sanjib, with an arrogant look on his face, asked, "So what?"

Nara got even more animated, "So what? It means he has a substantial and intimate knowledge of the local dialect of NE Sudan and eastern Chad. It isn't something he picked up in a school. It's like someone here from Everett or Somerville saying during a snowstorm, 'It's snowin' like a bastid.' What the hell does that mean? To 99% of the people, it is nonsense but to a local, it's a perfectly understandable and clear statement. He is local, to the Sudan. He is interesting, very interesting."

THE LIBRARY AGAIN

Joe was lucky. As a consultant to this project, he wasn't doing any of the heavy lifting. That would fall on the shoulders of Kevin and Sanjib's teams. They had milestones to meet, and he didn't. They had people to hire and manage, and he was a team of one. This being his first civilian job, however, he did need to prove himself. He spent a lot of time in the libraries researching terrain and refractivity and the latest developments in sensor and drone development. He tried hard to convince himself that his time was being spent there purely for serious reasons, but he couldn't help gazing at Lexi every chance he got. They had started dating shortly after their first meeting in the library, and the relationship kept building slowly but steadily from there.

It has been a long time since he had feelings like this for a woman. What would have been his soulmate for life was killed in her home country of Sudan for declaring her love for and intention to marry him. He was out of her tribe, religion, and race, and she had to pay the price for disgracing her family and tribe. It left him emotionally scarred, the deciding factor in his leaving the employ of the CIA. He honored the balance of his contract, and then came home to start a new life.

Joe also tried to convince himself that his developing feelings for Lexi were real and that the attraction wasn't just physical. She was a college grad, spoke four languages fluently, and worked at Harvard University for God's sake! Her feelings for him appeared to be real as well. He used the excuse of local cultures, and she used the geology and topography to keep the conversation going, at least in the beginning. After their first few weekends together, things were more relaxed. They shared many of the same interests, and she was a great listener. This was important to him, as he had no one else to talk to.

Lexi introduced Joe to her boss Harold, one day in the library and promised to arrange a future lunch. Her boss knew a lot about the people, tribes, customs, and trade routes of ancient Africa. It had been his specialty for many years. Mansa Musa did come up occasionally.

As time went on Joe, too, became intrigued with where

Musa's fortune could have gone or, more importantly, where it could have been hidden. This interest became a near obsession. In the back of his mind was a fantasy idea of what that wealth could accomplish if it were in the right hands. Better women's health care, education, and protection from physical abuse were all thoughts floating through Joe's mind, all to honor his former love.

Skip had Joe investigating a few things at the libraries, too, regarding drone development. The guy was either brilliant or knew things that hadn't been shared with the broader team. While the Pokey project had to do with early visual recognition and analysis, it was possible the same technology platform could be used with other sensors. The higher speeds would allow computers to make an instantaneous and more accurate decision on whether a person of interest was within sight.

In any case, Lexi was drop-dead gorgeous! Weather be damned, when she walked into a room, things brightened up considerably! He wasn't completely blind to the pluses and minuses of her personality. There were times when she wasn't aware of him watching her when she would argue with other employees at the library. That behavior was surprising to Joe as it seemed out of character, but we all had bad days or things we were passionate about. It really didn't matter, because to him, she was always considerate and pleasant.

WASHINGTON D.C

Joe, on occasion, would visit Washington D.C. as part of this project. He was an early riser and made his way to the JetBlue terminal at Logan Airport in Boston to catch an early morning flight. He was surprised to see Lexi get out of an Uber just two minutes after him, pulling an overnight piece of luggage behind her, making a short trip as well.

"Well, what a surprise to see you here and so early in the morning," said a smiling Joe who walked over to greet her.

Lexi was surprised at this unscheduled meeting and replied with a smile and a kiss. "It's a surprise to me, too! Where are you off to?"

"Washington, D.C. to conduct more research. How about you?"

"Chicago, for an exhibition on African Art. Harold doesn't always like to attend these things, so he will send me in his place. For me, it's like playing hooky! After a few more minutes of chitchat, they kissed goodbye and went their ways to their respective gates. Joe thought it was odd that she didn't mention this to him at dinner a few nights before. He deliberately didn't tell her or others about his travel plans because of the nature of his business. She, on the other hand, was usually chattier about what she was doing.

Joe's flight arrived before nine a.m., and he spent the balance of the morning at the Library of Congress, researching terrain and mineral matters and whatever he could pick up on drone development. The Library of Congress is the national library of the United States. It's the largest library in the world and houses nearly forty million books in almost five hundred languages. Its total collection of materials exceeds one hundred and seventy-five million items, including millions of maps which are stored in fifteen miles of bookcases. Its main reading room is in a beautiful, marbled one-hundred-foot-tall rotunda, seating three hundred people. He could have spent the rest of the day there and, weeks of his time, but he had another meeting scheduled that afternoon.

He spent the afternoon at NSA with an old buddy from "special services" named Matt who had risen to department head of sensor development. Matt had left the special services group many years before Joe and had settled down in the metro D.C. area where he had married and had two kids. He was in his late forties, of Irish decent, six feet tall, and a little overweight as a result of the move to a desk job. Years ago, he could sport a beautiful flat-top haircut, but time marched on, and the best he could do now was to cut his hair real close or shave his head completely.

Joe smiled as he walked into Matt's office and said, "It's good to see you again, pal. You're looking prosperous!"

Matt grinned when he said, "It's nice to see you too, Joe. All cleaned up in fancy clothes and not smelling like who knows what. Times have changed, eh? What brings you to D.C.?"

"I'm hoping you can help me. I'm out of the service and consulting now, working on a project that will need advanced sensors for use on satellites and drones to make it worth continued funding. It looks like I'll be spending a lot of time at the Library of Congress and with you too. What's new in your world?"

"My world is changing every day and getting more closely tied to drones. We have come a long way since the days of the U2 spy plane and miles of printed photos. Sensors have become even more important. Today, there are spy satellites and drones everywhere, capable of incredible types of sight, smell, sound, and other evaluations. Have you heard the phrase 'SBL' yet?"

"No, I haven't. What does it mean?"

"It stands for 'Smaller, Better, and Longer.' That's the mantra. Smaller in size to fit on ever-shrinking drone footprints. You must have seen videos of military guys in the field releasing drones into the air the size of the balsa wood airplanes we played with as kids. That's old technology already. The 'better' is the fanatical requirement to improve the capability of what we're making so that our technology cannot be outsmarted or negated by the other guys. 'Longer' refers to flight time. Every extra minute in flight can be the difference between success or failure. You cannot believe the pressure we're under."

"It sounds interesting. My project has separate hardware and software teams working on it back in Boston, and it's primarily visual recognition only. I'm the real-world reference for the team."

"Our real-life experiences are history, almost comical. Let me give you an example. You and I spent a lot of time in caves and hiding behind walls, right? Ducking this and bobbing that. Not anymore. The new concept is to drop dozens of these small pre-programmed miniature drones from a mother drone for a thirty-minute hunt. They will be programmed to stay nine or so feet away from each other, so they aren't all pursuing the same guy and then identify and pursue a kill based on the other parameters that have been inputted.

"For example, they could be programmed to identify and attack purely on a visual recognition, or a specific language, or attack a warm body adjacent to a specific metal object like a rifle. If you don't care who you kill, identifying any warm body will do. Facial recognition has been developing quite rapidly but for now, it has its limitations. It can be overcome by wearing an opaque veil or mask with a few aluminum strands added to reflect the signal or the traditional cloth turban with similar reflective material included in the weave. With gas detection, you can analyze their breath, body odor, or urine if present on their clothing. The limiting factor will soon be the length of time the drone can hunt for and identify its kill. If it runs out of time, it self-destructs.

"Ten years ago, you would have sent a squadron of marines into a rebel-held town to drive them out and free up the city. Pretty soon, you'll be able to wipe out an identified area of terrorists without losing a single soldier. Larger drones can be programmed to look for specific heat sources or radio signals, and then take them out. This is pinpoint warfare."

Joe raised his eyebrows and said, "Wow! I imagine, as with everything else, there are spies everywhere looking to steal this technology."

"Absolutely. Standard operating procedure is a five-minute talk every staff meeting on just that subject. Remember, we're talking about technology that can be used in traditional military applications, traditional commercial applications like farming, mining and petroleum, and inter-planetary applications. Think Mars, for example. The technology is incredibly valuable."

Joe changed the subject, "Are dust and sand still as big a problem for us as it was when we were working in the area?"

"Yeah, it is. Big or small, you can't fly through or, in the case of all drones, over a dust storm, and some of the storms last for days. You can't see through them either. Aluminum salts or any conductive metals in the dust can reflect and absorb radar waves and, as a result, interfere with their transmission. Strong mineral presence in an area is a big problem too. Ditto with mountains and ravines. It sucks."

"What about satellites; are we still using them as much?"

"Almost as much. They are used for big-picture stuff

like missile launches or storm tracking. They can cover a lot of area compared to a drone, which can only stay in the air for anywhere from thirty minutes to a few hours. Some of the satellites can stay up forever. They obviously won't have the voice recognition or gas detection sensors on board, but they will have enhanced infrared and ultraviolet capabilities."

The afternoon was ending. After giving a tour of the facility, Joe begged off on dinner to catch a flight back home. He would be visiting Washington on a more regular basis now and promised to catch up with his buddy on his next visit. Joe sat in his coach seat for the one-hour flight home amazed by what he had been told that day.

THREE

Lexi's Boss

Joe joined Lexi at the Shawmut Club for lunch with her boss. The Shawmut Club of Boston is a private social club located on Commonwealth Avenue in Boston's Back Bay area. Boston is host to many private social clubs, some of them associated with the area's many universities. It was founded in 1842 as a gentlemen's club but now open to all sexes, colors, and creeds. All one needs is a little money and a sense of decorum to apply.

If one were blindfolded and brought to their front door, one might think he or she were in London, and with good reason. Many of the buildings in this area were erected shortly after the Americans declared their independence from Great Britain. It was a beautiful stone-faced building with granite stairs flanked by iron railings, complete with boot-scrapers guiding you to the large oak door. Upon arrival, visitors were greeted by a doorman who ushered them into the oak-paneled foyer. A concierge then brought them to the dining room, the reading room, or one of the many meeting rooms in the building. With the Fourth of July celebration a week away, the traditional decorations and music made for a festive mood.

Harold Winthrop was your typical Ivy League academian: bow tie, pastel colored shirt, tweed sport coat, old money haircut, and long British face. Old North Shore Yankee money to be more specific, first made in the China trade, but multiplied many times over in real estate transactions over the past one hundred and fifty years. He was in his late sixties or early seventies in age, but it was difficult to tell. These old Yankees aged quickly, but then aged well. Often in these prestigious schools, people tended to stick around past normal retirement age, because once they left their prestigious positions, they were just old men. He was the thirteenth generation old New England money. Often their endowments came with strings attached, including the funding of respectable positions for their own to call home. Joe was brought to a table where Harold and Lexi had arrived a few minutes earlier.

"Joe, nice to see you again for more than a nod and a hello." Harold smiled. "I hear you spent time working and living in Africa. Is it true?"

"Well, yes, time in northern Africa on government projects."

"It's fascinating that our three lives are all tied to Africa. It has been my specialty for the past thirty-four years, and Lexi has been my assistant for the past five years. Before we get too engrossed in conversation, let's order lunch." All placed an order for lunch in what must be one of Boston's most elegant eating areas. Harold continued, "What about your current job brings you to our library on a regular basis, other than Lexi?"

"It's researching the project I'm working on which is confidential, so I can't get into too much detail. Part of my responsibilities is to provide background info and data on the cultures, landscapes, etc. to the project team, and having lived and worked in the area is a big plus."

Lexi turned to Harold with a slight laugh and said, "Do you remember the blow-up at the trivia night at that bar we went to a few months ago in Somerville over the richest man in the world question? It was one of Joe's friends that created all the fuss."

"Oh yeah, who was Mansa Musa!" chortled Harold. "It's a great trivia question, and a wild story! Usually anyone who has heard the correct answer never forgets it. Ah, here we go." The waiter returned, and conversation continued as they enjoyed their mid-day meal.

"I'll bet," said Joe, leaning forward with an intense look on his face. "I'm intrigued by this, being somewhat familiar with the region. I had never heard of the guy before. Who was he?"

"Musa was the king of the Mali Empire in West Africa in the early 1300s. At that time, Mali produced at least half of the world's gold and a high percentage of its salt as well. It was rumored that gold grew like carrots in Mali! Today, they still produce ten to fifteen tons of gold per year, or half a billion dollars' worth. Two tons are produced the old-fashioned way, by burrowing straight down as much as sixty-five feet in a hole three feet wide! Can you imagine doing that? The heat!

"Anyway, he was a devoted Muslim, and one of the obligations of the faithful, if they can afford it, is to make the Hajj, or pilgrimage to Mecca, at least once in his life. He could afford it and so in 1324, off he went along with forty to fifty thousand servants, soldiers, cooks, slaves, candlestick makers, you name it, for the two-year trip. Two years!

"He also brought with him what is wildly estimated to be as much as two billion dollars in gold and some other amount of salt, jewels, etc. as gifts. He spent or gave away so much gold on the good things in life, he depressed the value of gold for decades. It must have been a wild trip!" Harold laughed and paused for a sip of wine.

"My friend also got upset that night when he saw a weird-looking guy in the crowd that he remembered from growing up in Africa. He called him a tiger child. Did you see him?"

"I don't remember seeing anyone like that. I think he got the name wrong. There are some people called children of the lion/gazelle who live in that general area. They were part of an ancient religious cult. I imagine they could be intimidating. I don't know why one would be in Boston."

"Well, he really spooked and pissed off my friend."

"Well, there are a bunch of them throughout the Sahel."

Joe had heard the name Sahel before but was only familiar with the eastern portion of it. It's the strip of land that divided the Sahara desert from the African jungle. It consists of grasslands one hundred to five hundred miles wide that run across central Africa, coast to coast. It was formerly the home to large populations of grazing animals, including gazelles, cheetahs, and lions. Climate change over the centuries reduced their presence in the region.

"So, is the Sahel the path that Musa took on his pilgrimage to Mecca?"

"Pretty much, as it is the flattest, driest, and safest direct route. It still took eight to twelve months to make the crossing."

"So, he left Mali with a fortune in gold, salt, and other goodies. What did he bring home?"

"According to legend, he brought home artisans, scholars, scribes, astronomers, scientists, and some small portion of the gold he left with. That, my friend, is another story for a later date. We must leave now as we have a three-p.m. meeting, and we can't be late. It has been nice to finally say more than hello to you, Joe." Harold signed for the bill, and they left the club.

Joe smiled and thanked Harold for his time and lunch and said, "I look forward to seeing you again." He had an even bigger smile for Lexi and said, "Bye, Lexi."

Joe walked toward Boylston Street to catch the subway while Harold and Lexi hailed a taxi.

Harold turned to Lexi and with a serious look on his face said, "An interesting fellow. Stay close to him. We may be able to help one another." That was an order she had every intention of following.

LEXI'S TRAVELS

Lexi's job occasionally had her travel to other parts of the USA. Her prime reason was always to attend some function on behalf of her position at Harvard. The functions were usually tied to a presentation on African-related topics or an exhibit opening at a museum. Once her official capacities had been taken care of, however, the rest of her time was hers, and no one needed to know how or where she spent it. Harold would often have her visit customers of his separate consulting business, paying her out-of-pocket costs and a commission on whatever transactions occurred.

No paper trail was ever created or desired by either party. Harold's consulting business was named Africol, a contraction of African collections. He would offer his services to authenticate African objects and, often, act as a commissioned broker in any transactions. The legality of much of this was questionable as many of the transactions were in cash.

This trip started at the Museum of Fine Arts in New York City. Harold asked Lexi to attend the opening of a presentation entitled Nile Art. From all accounts, the exhibit was a smash, and Lexi encouraged Harold to come see it as well. With the afternoon free, Lexi took the opportunity to visit the town of Manhasset on Long Island to meet with someone Harold had been in contact with regarding selling several items. His name was Omar Elgazi, a businessman from the Arabian Gulf region. To do this, she hired a car and driver for the afternoon. This served two purposes; the first was to save time as she had never driven to any part of Long Island before and the second was to make the proper impression on her potential customer.

The trip to Manhasset was an eyeful. Welfare housing on Manhattan's east side, middle-class housing in Queens, and more elegant spreads the further one ventured out on Long Island. Manhasset is a Native American word for "island neighborhood." It's ideally located on Long Island so that travel by train or expressway to the city or the beaches is relatively easy. Its picturesque town center has a children's playground and a large gazebo for summer concerts. There's a wide range of housing available, but it's from expensive to extremely expensive.

By the time she arrived at Mr. Elgazi's home, the houses had morphed into mini mansions of ten to fourteen rooms on one or more acres of manicured lawns, many fenced in with ornate gates in front. His home was no exception with the added feature of a security guard at the gate. The four white pillars in front of his brick and marble mansion served as modern-day lion's warning all to respect the power within. A doorman greeted Lexi at the front door and brought her to the outdoor garden at the rear of the home where she met Mr. Elgazi for the first time.

"Miss Chekov, welcome to my home. It's a pleasure to finally meet you after all the telephone calls. Harold said you were a beautiful young lady, and that's an understatement." Mr. Elgazi was about sixty-five years old and of

Egyptian origin and fluid residences. His thinning gray hair was slicked straight back. He was an imposing figure at more than six feet in height and three hundred pounds in weight. The weather was warm and pleasant that day, and he was dressed in a light-pink shirt and light slacks. A linen sport coat and penny loafers (sockless of course) finished the picture, contact lens included.

"Thank you for your kind words, Mr. Elgazi, and it too is a pleasure to meet you." Lexi was dressed for the occasion in an expensive business suit, medium-height heels, and a white blouse all of which screamed "money." Over her left arm hung a small and expensive purse and in her left hand, an expensive leather portfolio.

"Come, come, please step into my garden. I'm proud of it. And please call me Omar." He had every reason to be proud of it with its beautiful array of flowers, shrubs, and trees, some of which were exotic and unique on Long Island. They sat under a large white pergola that was over an intricate stone patio facing an antique bronze fountain. A servant brought glasses of iced tea for both.

"Harold was interested in a valuable stone you were interested in selling and asked me to pay you a visit to take a look at it and discuss other commercial matters," said Lexi to start the conversation.

"And I thank you and Harold for your time and interest and help in this matter. Your reputations precede you, and I'm comfortable working with both of you in this delicate matter." Mr. Elgazi then reached into his jacket pocket and pulled out a bulging velvet cloth purse. "This ruby has been in my family for more than four hundred years. Unfortunately, my relative, who must remain anonymous, has fallen on hard times and as much as they hate to do it, must sell this stone." He then passed the purse to Lexi for examination. It contained a large ruby with deep-red coloring and flawless composition.

"This is a beautiful stone. Can you tell me its history?" asked Lexi with an obvious look of approval on her face.

"I've been told it comes from ancient mines in India in a region known for its beautiful precious stones. I can't prove it other than comparing the coloring with other stones of that area. It was probably a standalone gem, perhaps hanging at the bottom of a gold chain."

"It has such an unusual cut to it, fascinating." Lexi recognized a 'con' when she saw one. She nodded to say I believe you, when in fact she had been in this business long enough to recognize a gem that had been pried from a crown during a restoration and replaced with a fake. Who would question one fake stone among the many real ones? Who would accept that responsibility and liability?

"It's very beautiful, and I can understand the great reluctance of your relative in parting with it, but the realities of the world often step in and force our hands. I'm not sure what I can do for you. There are several prestigious jewelers and auctioneers who would be pleased to handle such a sale for you at a lower commission than we would charge. It's not that I'm trying to turn away business, but it's important that we trust each other. I wouldn't want you to be upset if you felt we had been anything but fair and open with you," said Lexi with a healthy dose of cool European reserve.

This was all part of the dance international art and

jewelry thieves go through at the beginning of a negotiation. If this had been Omar's first sale, he may have bought Lexi's line, but it was not. He appreciated the validating ritual and responded to Lexi accordingly, "I thank you for your honesty, and appreciate that excellence must be duly rewarded. Complicating this transaction will be the matter of accrued back taxes that I expect would consume most of the proceeds. We have the additional challenge of explaining how the jewel left its home country without it being duly recorded." Omar raised his eyebrows and rocked his head back and forth a few times, emphasizing the delicacy of this matter.

The action had returned to Lexi for the next volley. "I understand your difficulties, and I think we can help you with the utmost of discretion as we have done so with others in the past."

"Thank you."

Lexi swung into negotiation mode. "We have many customers of great wealth who may be interested in this beautiful stone. Like your relative, they prefer anonymity and cash transactions through friendly countries to avoid taxation and other formalities. Harold said you feel this stone is worth between two and three million dollars. Of course, we would have it independently assessed by one of our associates, and the buyer will do the same. Our commission on a sale like this will be twelve percent of the ultimate selling price with ownership of the stone passing directly from you to the buyer. You'll need to price our commission into the selling price of the stone. All payments and legal work will occur outside of the United States for simplicity and, as you say, tax reasons."

"I understand. How quickly could you begin the process?"

"The next step is yours. You need to tell us what your asking price is, including a small margin for negotiation and other incidental costs that could creep into the deal, and our commission. If we feel it is a reasonable price to ask, we will proceed. We don't want to make any false promises or create bad feelings by undertaking a project that we feel has no chance of success. If we're both on the same page, we can begin our work after receipt of the first third of our commission, or approximately one hundred and twenty thousand dollars." Lexi could see his eyes wince just a bit with this requirement.

"Well, let me think about this for a few days. That's a lot of money upfront for no guarantee of success, young lady."

"You're a senior businessman who has had to deal with recruiting talent over the years. It's not easy and when you had a need for a critical position, chances are you relied on a retained recruiter to do the job. They got paid in steps to get the job done, including an upfront payment to go out and search forth. We're the same. I assume you've spoken with some of our customers who are all pleased with our work. If you haven't, I can provide you with several to contact."

"I understand you, and the recruiting analogy is a good one. Please give me a few days to think this over and come up with a few more questions or suggestions. Who knows!" At this point, Omar smiled and reached across the table and clinked his glass with Lexi. He took a sip of iced tea and quietly leaned back in his chair for a full minute.

With a serious look on his face, he sat upright and said, "I have something else I want to show you." He then reached behind and to the side to remove a burlap sack from a solid lawn object. It was a stone carving of a falcon, three feet high and two feet wide. The workmanship was excellent. Wear and tear indicated it wasn't a new carving. Lexi wasn't prepared for this item and got up from her chair to look it over. "Tell me about it."

"This falcon is from the recent diggings at Thebes and is three thousand years old, from the Middle dynasty. I went to great expense to get this out of Egypt. Now I need to find a private collector of great discretion for it. It's very unique, and I can't quite put a value on it. What I would like you to do pro bono is determine its desirability and price. Of course, when matters proceed to where we are with the ruby, we would formalize the relationship."

"I will, of course, report this back to Harold tomorrow, or the next day at the latest. This, too, is an interesting object of art." After a little small talk and finishing her iced tea, Lexi said, "Well, if there's nothing else we need to discuss today, I'll head back into the city."

"We're finished for now, but please stay. May I take you to lunch or even dinner? We have many good restaurants in this area. Name your cuisine," he said with a smile and an outstretched hand.

"Thank you, but I have another meeting later this afternoon in Manhattan. I'm sorry, perhaps the next time," said a polite Lexi.

"Of course, but you need to have lunch. Please join me for a quick lunch here on the patio. I'll have the kitchen prepare something quick and then you can be on your way with at least a little food in your stomach. Twenty minutes, that's all."

She didn't want to appear rude and would need something before her next meeting, so she agreed and had a salad with him. With her car on call, she thanked Omar and got in to make the return trip to Manhattan. The next meeting would be special, part personal and part business. It was with Michael.

The return ride to her hotel in Manhattan took longer than anticipated but still had her back in her room by three-thirty in the afternoon. This was enough time for her to rest her eyes for two hours and shower and dress up for her seven o'clock meeting. Michael was an old friend from the Ukraine. He was the one who looked out for her when she was in need. He was the one who arranged for her student visa to the USA and her green card for permanent residency. He was her first lover.

Their friendship went back to Lexi's high school days. He was a junior administrator in the local social services office and ten years older than she. Neither had any money, and whenever they were together, they would walk to their destination or grab a bus. It didn't matter; they were young. His government contacts provided the visas and such to free Lexi from her impoverished life. She was in love with him and assumed he felt the same way about her. Other forces were in play, however, and their paths parted as Michael was frequently transferred within the Soviet Union and even overseas, like now. They continued to stay in touch with one another and would occasionally get together for an evening. It was coincidental that they would both be in Manhattan at the same time. They met at her upscale Eastside hotel, The Parkston.

"Hello Lexi, you look ravishing as always," said Michael, extending his hands but then separating and putting both arms around Lexi for a hug. Lexi closed her eyes and gave him a squeeze. Michael could be described as "continental" versus "Russian." He was six feet tall with a closely trimmed head of black hair. His clothes were continental as were his shoes. He had rugged good looks one might expect of a Ukrainian Cossack and the charm of a diplomat. His 'come hither' eyes were framed by a slight tan.

"Hello Michael, handsome as ever." They held hands and leaned back for a second to admire one another and then took a seat in the hotel's main bar, Trafalgar. In the concrete jungle that's Manhattan, the wood-paneled dimly lit Trafalgar was a trip to places far away.

"So, how are you doing, my love?" asked Michael.

"I'm doing fine, thank you. And you?" Lexi was a little anxious and hoped it didn't show.

"I'm living the life, as you Americans say, but seeing a bit too much of the world right now." He had remained in Russia after the breakup of the Soviet Union and had worked his way to "officially" a senior position in the Ministry of Energy. Energy was global, and he was seeing most of it firsthand. "How is your boss treating you? Is he behaving well?"

"Yes, we're getting along fine. So, tell me, are you still single?"

"Still single with no prospects in sight. And you?"

"The same," said Lexi with a slight and sympathetic smile on her face.

It had been awhile since they had seen each other and rather than moving on to dinner, they remained in the bar. They talked for hours, at times laughing, and at other times, engaged in serious discussion. As time wore on, they both mellowed, and the conversation became more metered and endearing. The evening was at a junction point, too late and too drunk for dinner, and too early to call it a night. They chose a path that led to her hotel room and a night of romance. Michael left at six the following morning, and Lexi at ten, both promising to stay in touch. At mid-day, it was a short taxi to LaGuardia airport and the shuttle back to Boston. She was back in the office by two pm, filling Harold in on the business parts of her visit. That evening in her apartment, she would sit alone and as she always did after a rendezvous with Michael, still wondering if their occasional relationship would ever amount to anything.

VISIT TO NSA

It was time for another visit to Washington, D.C. as part of the project. Joe made good on his promise to Matt to not only see him but accept his invitation to spend the night at his home with his family. Much had happened in the intervening months, and he now had other things he was interested in pursuing in addition to Pokey, like finding Musa's gold and putting it to good use.

"I've been doing more project research on sensors and have a few questions for you, Mister Expert."

"I'm listening," replied Matt.

"Okay. Today's questions are:

1. How far below the earth's surface can you detect metals and oil?
2. Can you detect infrared and ultraviolet light?
3. Can you beam infrared or ultraviolet light down to earth and cause things to glow?
4. What about smell?"

"Question number one depends on a number of variables like the altitude we're measuring from, the material we're measuring, and the soil we're penetrating. For gold, titanium, silver, steel, etc., three feet below the surface. Ditto with land mines, if that's what you're thinking. We can also detect voids, like tunnels. We can go deeper in sand and even deeper in water, which is where oil comes into the equation. Regarding number two, yes we can read both, but you need to be aware that urban areas or military bases can block everything out.

We can beam down both lights, but only by using low flying drones and within a range of a few feet. Smell is highly confidential. I hear there's a lot of work going on in that area. 'Smell' is an odor, and an odor is a gas. The compounds of a gas can already be detected. Smell could be sweat, urine, feces, or bad breath. Sweat or urine analysis could tell you what the person had eaten. It could also detect a dead body."

"If I give you several areas to scan, can you give me a few readings?"

"Sure."

"Great! Okay, fifteen degrees south of the equator to thirty degrees north, thirty degrees west of Greenwich to forty-five degrees east."

"Ah, the old stomping grounds. Did you leave your wallet there? This will have to be by satellite and it's too big an area to scan in one pass. You'll see nothing. Cut it into much smaller slices and then look."

"Okay. Three slices:

1. Twenty degrees west to fifteen degrees east, twenty degrees to thirty degrees north.
2. Fifteen degrees west to forty-five degrees east, ten degrees north to twenty degrees north.
3. Zero degrees to forty-five degrees east, seven degrees north to seven degrees south.

"I would like individual scans with UV, IR, and whatever it takes to look for gold, titanium, silver, steel, whatever you can give me. I'm not sure what to expect, so if there are shaded areas, let me see that as well."

"Boy, you're not asking for much. Okay, give me a week to get things lined up. Some of the satellites circle the earth every ninety minutes while others take much longer, and some may need to be moved which could require permission. If it does, what do I tell my superiors?"

"Tell them it's all part of a top-secret program under development, and they can call me with any questions. And, thank you." Joe was sure Matt would follow through. With nothing being said, both remembered Joe saving his friend's life, and he owed Joe a big one.

Dinner that evening with Matt's wife Cindi and the kids was very enjoyable. They lived in Falls Church, Virginia, a beautiful and now expensive suburb of Washington, D.C. Joe had known Cindi since she and Matt were dating, and he had attended their wedding some ten years ago. He was envious of the happiness they had found together and Matt's decision to get out of the intelligence business much earlier than he. The evening passed quickly and, after a quick breakfast the following morning with Matt and Cindi, Joe was back on a plane and headed home.

Mount Washington

Four months into the project, and things were in general still progressing well. The facility was being cleaned up and modernized, and equipment was being received and installed. Much effort was being expended on recruiting the necessary technical staff, especially programmers. This was a challenge because many claims were made for technical prowess but when put to the test, practical experience quickly failed. Complicating all of this were Sanjib and Skip's "type A" personalities which combined to chase away several promising candidates. Joe and Lexi's relationship had continued to develop to a much more involved and intimate level.

Joe and Lexi left her apartment in Cambridge bright and early at six a.m. one Saturday morning for the five-hour drive north through New Hampshire to the White Mountain National Forest. They had spent previous weekends camping in various places in New England but were now going to the "big leagues." Among the crown jewels of the seven hundred and fifty-one-thousand-acre wilderness are the Flume, the Kancamagus Highway, and Mount Washington. It's the highest mountain peak in the northeast United States. Mt. Washington's climate is alpine, with low temperatures and very high winds, limiting the top thirteen hundred feet to scrub bushes, tundra, and algae. On top of the mountain is a manned weather observatory which on an afternoon in April 1934, recorded the highest observed wind speed ever on earth, two hundred and thirty-one miles per hour. The weather is quite unpredictable and often catches climbers off-guard and unprepared for the worst.

Snow and bad weather in general have caused the majority of the more than one hundred and fifty deaths that have occurred on the mountain since records have been kept. When the weather is good and the sky is clear, the view extends all the way to the ocean, Canada, and New York State! You can drive to the top or take the world-famous cog railway, or be a purist, and hike it.

At eleven a.m., they arrived at the cog railway train base and parked for the two-day trip. Unlike many trips, hiking in the White Mountains is more vertical than horizontal. You're usually following mountain streams or climbing hand over hand and around rocks. After a quick lunch, they followed the A trail for five hours all the way up to the Lake of the Clouds hut. The Lake of the Clouds is a small glacial pond that formed in a basin at approximately the five-thousand-foot elevation. There's an Appalachian Mountain Club hut here that can handle ninety campers overnight on bunk beds, providing dinner and breakfast, warmth and bathrooms. It's as close to the summit as you can get before camping down for the night.

"Wow, it's beautiful up here. Is this where we're staying tonight?" asked an excited and a little out of breath Lexi.

"No, I'm not sleeping here with a bunch of granola heads or singing Kumbaya. We're going further up and out of sight to the tundra near Tuckerman Ravine. This is where I used to camp when I was a kid. It's illegal now but screw it. Sandwiches and trail mix will have to do." Lexi scowled slightly, but off they went.

They hiked and huffed and puffed for another forty-five minutes until Lexi found a relatively flat place protected by a few large boulders. Down below, and to the west, was the hut. To the east was the dangerous Tuckerman Ravine. The sun was going down, and they spread out their sleeping bags and had dinner. Dinner was sandwiches and hard-boiled eggs, as they couldn't risk a fire being seen and subsequent arrest. It was all washed down with ice-cold water pulled from a stream hours earlier.

There were a few small rocks interfering with Lexi's attempt to have a flat place to sleep. She removed most of them, and now had a flat place to lie down. It was an incredible view, and more so later with shooting stars galore in the crystal-clear sky. In the distance was an occasional village light. The muted sound of train whistles from distant valleys punctuated the nighttime silence. It was the perfect time and place to do some "exploring" of each other.

"So how many other girls have you brought here?" probed a slyly smiling Lexi.

"None, you're the first," replied Joe, without a return smile. As Lexi would find out, Joe was serious when it came to discussing his relationships.

"Really?"

"Really. I used to come here with my fraternity brothers and friends. No girls." After a slight pause, Joe spoke again, "You know, you have hiker's legs. Did you ever climb mountains while living in the Ukraine?"

"Well, we would hike trails, but nothing like this. The terrain wasn't as bleak or as strenuous. What do you mean hiker's legs?"

"You don't say much about living in the Ukraine. What was it like? Did you have many friends or family?"

"You know, the usual. I had a mother and a father and a younger brother and sister. Mom was a seamstress, and Dad and my brother worked on a farm. A lot of love but little money."

"Are they still alive? Do you ever see them?"

"Oh yes, they are still alive. Things are pretty tight. Dad is still working, even though he should have stopped. My brother was injured in an accident and is in a wheelchair in an institution. Little sister got married, but to a bad guy. She has a little girl. I went back three years ago to see them."

"Did anyone else in your family go to college?"

"No, just me. I had very good grades, and I wanted to get away. It was very depressing to me. What do you mean, hiker's legs?"

"Your legs are very shapely from exercising, either hiking or biking. Shapely legs that go with a nice butt, tight stomach, nice boobs, a pretty face and hair, and a neck that whispers kiss me, you fool." And with that comment, Joe slipped into Lexi's sleeping bag for the night. After sex, she quickly fell asleep. Joe rolled over on his back and stared at the stars in the sky for the longest time. At that precise moment, all should have been good in the world, but as much as he tried to fight the feeling, he knew something wasn't quite right.

Joe had been lonely often. Music would be one of his few steady companions over the years. A song would get stuck in his brain and play over and over until it would often drive him to an outburst of some kind. All it took were a few key lyrics and the right "sound," and it was stuck there, for years. Tonight was "Under the Milky Way" by the group Church. There were things in his growing relationship with Lexi that didn't square with his idea of reality. *What was she looking for?*

At sunrise the next morning, they broke camp to get back to the trail and head to the top of the mountain where they could get a hot breakfast. Although it was August, the temperature was a crisp thirty-nine degrees and the sky a deep blue.

"How did you sleep?" inquired Joe, who had gotten up ten minutes earlier than Lexi and was packing for the hike to the summit.

"Once you got off me, pretty well, outside of a few small stones that pinched my back and neck."

"Are you complaining?"

"No, not at all. This has been a wonderful experience." As Lexi rolled up her sleeping bag, she picked up the two small stones that had hurt her back and threw them aside. She noticed something slightly shiny in their place. She moved some pebbles and dirt to reveal a silver dollar that someone placed and covered under the stone. With a little extra effort, more silver coins were found set in a side-by-side formation. All the coins were American and from the 1920s.

"Look at this, how cool! Two silver dollars, two half dollars, two quarters, and two dimes. Why would anyone do this?"

"I don't know," replied Joe, now looking at the handful of coins. "People must have camped here before. They were put there for a reason. Someone planned to come back sometime later to celebrate an anniversary or something. Maybe it was parents and kids. Judging from the dates, it was probably sometime in the 1930s or 1940s."

"Hmmm, then I'll cover them up and leave them in place. They must have had a special meaning, or it was a promise. Only the people who placed them here would know enough to come looking for them. We can check back in every few years." Lexi then put them back just as she found them.

The hike to the top of the mountain was completely on a rocky path. One hour later, they had made it, huffing and puffing in the even thinner air. The temperature had climbed to fifty degrees. Warmed up by the hike was encouragement to remove a layer of clothing, which revealed the delicious curves of Lexi's body. Interrupting all of this was the arrival of a car that had just made the ten-mile circuitous climb on the toll road from the eastern base.

"Whew, we made it!" said a chubby ten-year-old that had jumped out of the car's backseat. They smiled and watched as the cog railroad train made its descent to its base camp on the west of the mountain. They too would need to begin the descent soon, as it was surprisingly as strenuous going down the hill as up. The five-hour drive home was quiet as both were exhausted by the weekend's exercise. Lexi snuggled into Joe's shoulder for much of the long drive home.

FOUR

NSA Satellite Report

"You had best come here again to review the results," beckoned Matt at the NSA. "The exact coordinates you gave me were too broad but by trimming them a bit, I was able to get some good results. It's interesting that there were some faint UV signals where there were also faint precious metals signals. It might have to do with altitude. The tests were also conducted over several days, and they weren't always repeatable."

"Could you use your best judgement and trim the scan areas a little further to see if it produces better results?"

"Sure, I can probably do it now. It will take a few more passes. I'll give you a call when done. The satellites are still in place. It should take no more than a day. I'm curious—why this interest?"

"I'm interested in where the caravans may have gone. There may be high-altitude water or paths we're not aware of."

Joe returned to Washington, D.C. two days later to discuss the further findings.

"Not much more to show," said Matt. "Salts show up everywhere, which is no surprise in the desert areas, and urine is big on the trade routes. What are unusual are the trace featherings going to higher ground; maybe they were trade routes in the past, or they camped at higher grounds for safety. In any case, I've made prints of the various satellite swatches you can take back to Boston."

This confirmed what Joe had been thinking. Bodily fluids show up well under UV light. Caravans of all kinds including Musa's could have reached much higher ground than previously thought. Once home, Joe continued his analysis. *Thank God for the National Geographic*, he thought as he overlaid the various mapping strips Matt gave him on to his National Geographic maps of the region. It was intriguing that the signals (as weak as they were) came from near the tops of major mountains, as did the precious metals signals. The UV light received could be the result of prisms, and the salt scans were the result of beaming UV light down.

The salt scans weren't as definitive as many deserts are full of salt deposits, especially in northern Africa. A large part of Musa's fortune was due to his incredible salt deposits. Joe wasn't looking for salt mines; he was looking for well-worn travel routes. It was the overlay of the trace chemicals that, while scattered, brought things into focus. The trace mineral scan was primarily along the caravan paths as expected.

What was surprising were the frays or feathers that

veered off inexplicably and usually to higher grounds. The caravans normally moved to higher, drier, and safer grounds for camping, but many of them proceeded to even higher mountainous grounds. The feathering and trace mineral scans added flesh to the bones of a developing image. Joe tried to tie together in his mind all the strange things that he had encountered about northern Africa in the past few months:

Musa and his five hundred-billion-dollar fortune

These UV and precious metals signals of northern Africa

On top of this, he remembered Lexi finding the old coins under a rock high up on Mount Washington and her comment, "Only those people who put them here would know to look for them here." He knew there was a connection but couldn't quite figure it out yet. It was time to consider high-tech tests of a few primitive codes.

REMOUNT

The summer had come and gone, and fall was closing in. Skip and Joe were invited to a project review meeting in Washington, D.C. While there, they were told they were being added to a broader top-secret project that would expand the work of their project. Pokey would be the platform for the next generation of military reconnaissance sensors. Word of the Pokey project had leaked, and now the Chinese and Russians were initiating similar efforts. As a result, security for the project would be tightened. This had

Joe reviewing in his mind anything he may have said to Lexi or her boss or anyone else.

Apparently and in separate projects, sensor and drone developments had made a few breakthroughs (*The rumors were true*, thought Joe). With drones, miniaturization was paying off in a big way. Micro-miniature motors were paving the way for hummingbird and dragonfly-size drones to target individuals with small-caliber bullets or contact explosives. Further down the road were bumblebee-size drones with the same capability, and way down the road and really in the realm of fantasy and science fiction were mosquito-size drones able to infect one person with a poison, after which the injection would start a chemical reaction that would cause the bug to burn up and vaporize.

Additional development work was progressing nicely on advanced three-dimensional facial mapping and chemical gas recognition, i.e. sweat, breath, urine, etc. A hummingbird-size drone could fly around a room in complete darkness, looking for a match against someone's chemical map, and if a match was found, use their IR sensor to locate and take the appropriate action.

This would be neat, clean, and with no loss of American life. Voice recognition, already used commercially by mutual funds as an additional step against fraud, was also being further developed. Work on enhanced cameras continued as well. All these new weapons would need advanced hardware and software, i.e. Pokey.

Additionally, the R&D team needed to determine whether this effort could be assisted by powerful radar stations located at or near the top of remote mountain locations in the North African region. These stations and satellites would gather and retransmit data and provide a one-two punch. Since Joe had previous assignments in the region, as well as speaking Arabic and some of the other regional languages, would he be open to assisting the team evaluating the proposed sites? Joe agreed to "assist" without specifying any limits. His background had obviously been made available to some people, but how many, and why?

Joe knew the region's terrain could be a problem. Unlike the mountains most Americans and Europeans were used to, which are primarily made of granite or other hard stones, some of these African mountains look like moonscapes with rubble rock, sandstone, and silica dust all the way to the top.

Both men returned home pleased with the results of the meetings. Skip was happy he would have greater responsibilities, an increase in pay and most importantly, years of work ahead of him with the current and anticipated workloads. Joe, on the other hand, was relieved that his settling down in Cambridge looked like it would stay, regardless of how much "assistance" he supplied.

THE TEST

The fall and winter months flew by quickly, and the weather was getting colder week by week. Initial product testing at CML began shortly after the installation and debugging period, which lasted five months. The lab had been designed so that continuous upgrading could happen as newer/better/faster equipment became available. Since this was a secret military project, there was every incentive to keep pushing new development and write off its costs well ahead of it going into commercial service several years later.

It was time again for one of Skip's monthly meetings. With everyone present and seated, he said to the group in his usual abrupt fashion, "Okay people, this month's update," and with an outstretched forefinger pointed, said, "Sanjib, you're first... Go!"

"Okay, we've made good progress in hiring programmers. Ten are on board, with three more to go. The two that quit weren't going to work out anyway because they wouldn't take direction. My thanks go out to Mildred and her team for finding this talent and bringing them onboard. We're also making good progress in increasing capture speeds and ratios. It would be nice to pause for a while so we could document more at any one set of frequencies, map out performance, and minimize distortion. In any case, good progress is being made."

"Hold it right there, bucko." Skip could flash to anger quickly, "For the hundredth time in thirteen months, we need to wow the military and intelligence community with where we are and what we have produced and have a solid argument to ask for more funding. Goddamn it, I'm sixty-one years old and do not want to be a store greeter or sell paint at a hardware store. We're not pausing for anything. Take advantage of every hardware or software upgrade you can. We must stay ahead of the Russians and Chinese. Keep pushing! You got it?"

"Yah, boss," replied Sanjib, flashing his eyes and slightly shaking his head in silent disapproval.

Skip then turned and asked, "Joe, what's new?"

"I'm in regular contact with Washington and am looking for more data and analysis on mineral/metals detection, and dust. There continues to be concern over the absorption and reflection of some of the rocks and minerals. There are a lot of salts in this region, and it affected some sensor capabilities, worse so during the many dust storms. I've been to the local university tech libraries, as well as New York City and D.C., but feel I need to tap into other databases, in other languages. I'll let you know what I come up with."

"No boondoggles. Keep it cheap. I'll need a report," warned Skip.

"I understand. Everything will get your approval."

"Okay, Kevin, what's up?"

"Things are moving along nicely. I too want to compliment Human Resources' assistance in recruiting. Thanks to their help, we're fully staffed. To Sanjib's point, we're looking to get higher quality/tighter tolerance components to minimize distortion. We shouldn't be getting this much distortion on our displays. I think part of our project charter should be writing and re-writing specifications as we learn more. This will be valuable as we move forward and on other projects as well. We need to get credit for doing this. This will require extra time and money. How do we get that approved?"

"Good idea, Kevin. Let me bounce it up the chain for approval," said Skip. "I'm sure the higher ups will see value in this. Mildred?"

"Recruiting efforts continue, with some difficulty. We're a bit more demanding than other companies and our location here in an unattractive building and part of town is a negative. The money is good, however, and we will keep on with our efforts."

"Thank you, Mildred," said Skip. "Bob?"

"Nothing major to report. Year to date, we're slightly under budget regarding people. You all may notice it's a little cold in here and that's because the facility upgrades are a little behind schedule. I have meetings set with several of the contractors next week and will delay payments until they get back on schedule."

Skip looked around the room and asked, "Anything else?" No one spoke up. "Apparently not, meeting adjourned."

HAROLD'S INTERVIEW

Joe arranged for a second meeting with Harold, this time for dinner. Although Joe wanted to pay for it, due to timing and convenience, Harold insisted it be on campus at one of the private dining rooms reserved for faculty and their guests. Like many of the buildings on campus, it was made of brick and in the Georgian style which was in vogue in England and the colonies three hundred years ago.

It was much like the Shawmut Club with its expensive wood paneling and paintings on the wall of people long gone from this world but remembered still in the cities and towns that graced their names, or the university endowments they made. Christmas was around the corner and fresh snow on the ground complemented the decorations all around Harvard Square where, as always, there were many people scurrying on their way to shops, study, or evening entertainment.

After being escorted to a table and ordering a drink and dinner, Harold asked, "So, what's new?"

"Well, the usual. Work is proceeding at a pace you would expect for a government project. It can get boring, but it pays the bills. Thanks for asking. I appreciate you finding time to meet with me again. I asked you for dinner because I've done a lot of research, and I'm intrigued by the Mansa Musa story."

"It has become a siren song of sorts for some. Just the crumbs off his table would propel a person into the realm of the super wealthy," replied a serious Harold in an almost sonorous and theatrical tone of voice.

"What do you think happened to the gold?" asked Joe.

"Keep in mind that his was a two-year trip so things had a chance to develop and be modified. Everywhere the king stopped, he bought and traded. He lavished gifts on his hosts and greased a few palms to guarantee safe passage even though it's rumored he traveled with twelve thousand foot soldiers. He brought with him religious types, doctors, scholars, astrologers, quite a travelling troop of heavy thinkers. So, while he is travelling along and paying for most things in gold, he continued to cheapen its value as it was no longer as precious.

"By the time he got to Mecca and had been there awhile, word was probably getting back to him that people back in Egypt and Sudan and other places were getting pretty upset that the value of his gift, or the price he paid for something, continued to fall. That was bad press, not to mention he would eventually retrace his steps through what could now be or quickly become hostile territories.

"I think he summoned his top thinkers to figure out a way to minimize the damage, and that was to stop paying for things in gold, and start by paying in other precious minerals, jewels, or other products like salt. It was documented that he took out gold-based loans and bought back some of the gold to help prop up its price. That was a smart move, but now he was stuck with it on the trip home."

"Okay, it makes sense. What makes you think this is what happened?" was Joe's reply.

"There's no indication in any African literature I've read in the past thirty odd years that indicates that the gold moved south, and the north was the desert. The damage that was done was local to the disbursement. Of the rumored two billion dollars of gold he brought with him, one half was disbursed by the time prices started to fall. He started his trip home with one billion dollars' worth of gold."

"That's still a lot of money. What did he do with it?"

"I think he brought some back to Mali, but he probably arranged to have most of it hidden on the return home. The billion-dollar question is where? Now that I've told you my story, you're more familiar with the region than you can admit. I'll finish my salad while you tell me where you think he hid it?"

"If I knew, you would be asking someone else that question because I would be long gone." Joe smiled. "I haven't a clue but would start with asking 'where', 'why', and 'how'. It would have to be a place where he and his advisors felt it was safe and secure from others and difficult to retrieve. How would you keep his slaves and soldiers from talking if they knew where it was hidden?

"My guess is that the gold is hidden along the reverse route in the Sahel or higher and not the jungle below where too many eyes would be aware of what was going on. Vegetation and swamps would make retrieval very difficult over time, let alone help identify where they had put it.

"The logistics would also need to be considered. A strong camel could carry ten million dollars in gold or one hundred camels one billion dollars in gold. Plus, you have all the attendant people. Logistically, hiding, let alone moving, this amount of gold seems impossible. How it was hidden and remained so for all of these years is the biggest unknown."

"Interesting observations with which I agree," said Harold. "I think for the return home, small groups of camels would need to be arranged every so many weeks apart. Remember, the return trip was 365 days, so they had plenty of time to hide the goods. Of course, after hiding the gold, all the attendants were probably killed."

"But that's only one plus billion of his five hundred billion dollars in gold. What happened to the balance?"

"Again, I don't know. It was recorded that the empire fell into chaos after Mansa Musa's death some years after his return home. Stealing or moving one half-trillion dollars in gold would have been difficult and traceable. There's no record of that. He might have hidden that gold as well. If he did, there must have been an extensive and sophisticated plan in place to retrieve all or some of it. A misstep could be disastrous. I'm sure that woven among the many tales told by the storytellers lay the truth, but finding it is the challenge."

"I've read everything I could find locally on this subject. Where else might I find more?"

"You can try the Library of Congress or maybe the Metropolitan Library in New York City. Your best chances might be in Europe, Paris, because Mali eventually became a French possession, or Cairo, or even London because the British were poking around parts of Africa as well. Maybe go to Mali itself or the Vatican or wherever there's a religious library. I don't know what else to tell you. If you do pursue this further, please be sure to share what you find with Lexi and me. We are very interested." Between questions and discussion, they were able to finish dinner.

The waiter brought an after-dinner drink to the two of them. Changing subjects, Harold asked, "How are you and Lexi getting along? She seems to be quite taken by you."

"We're doing fine. I like her, too. How long has she worked for you?"

"Oh, it's been almost six years now. Her first job at Harvard was for someone else, but to my good fortune, she quickly got transferred to my department. She's a good girl, a bright girl, and in some ways, an enigma to me. If suddenly she told me she could speak ten languages, or flap her arms and fly, I would believe her. So much talent."

"Have you ever met her family?"

"No, not a soul. They are all back in the Ukraine. She's all alone in the States. Treat her well; she's a keeper." After their drink, the men gathered their belongings and prepared to leave. With a handshake at the door and a promise to stay in touch, they walked in opposite directions to their respective homes in the brisk evening air.

JOE THINKS

It was one of those nights where thoughts were nursed by a drink or two. Sitting in a comfortable chair in a seventh-floor apartment overlooking the Charles River and the Boston skyline was conducive to deep and sometimes therapeutic thinking. Intellectual pondering was easy, handling emotional demons was not.

There were few people in the world who knew the heights and depths of this region better than Joe, thanks to his long service to the US intelligence services.

His access to surveillance satellites, and now both advanced satellites and drones, made him even more unique. If even a fraction of this golden fortune were recoverable, Joe could move forward with the long-standing personal commitment he made to improve the lives of the women in this region.

As a result of his dinner earlier that evening with Harold, he thought even more about how and where to hide a few billion dollars of gold, from a fourteenth-century perspective. It wouldn't be in the jungle area because of the swamps, vegetation, and excess of people. Diseases were too many and too easy to catch in these areas. Critical people/links could die in an instant. He would hide it in the Sahel or higher. The land was dry and accessible but again, you have the problem of too many eyes. The solution might be to move to ever-higher grounds.

There would be fewer eyes but at some point, the altitude and terrain would hinder you. As a member of a secret team placing satellite transmission stations in obscure locations, he was familiar with some of the highest terrains. Much of that landscape looked like the surface of the moon. Some hadn't been climbed by Europeans until the early part of the twentieth century. That's how remote they were. Some were in war zones, making climbing more challenging. He reviewed in his mind what the strangest sites were like.

Although they resembled a moon-like terrain, for some reason, most had several pieces of hand-cut wood near the top and off the beaten path. Some were in positions that would be difficult to retrieve, mostly buried among or wedged in stones. They were unlikely to be placed there for firewood. Had there been a house or building of some type there at one time? The team thought it was odd, but they had more important things to think of, like getting out of there alive.

Working was made far more difficult by the altitude. Although acclimated to higher altitudes, they brought oxygen just in case. Most people weren't aware of the mountains in Africa over twelve thousand feet high and snowbound for much of the year. The cold, the difficulty in breathing, and working at that altitude created special requirements for the workers.

How do you limit the number of people who could access it? How do you keep a secret? Do you have several people each with a piece of the puzzle or a turn of the lock (as with Swiss bank accounts?

Now he started to think gold. How high could a camel go and still work, effectively carrying hundreds of pounds of gold or supplies? How would they stay warm? How high could a person work without oxygen tanks?

How high can jungle types go? How would you start a fire to cook or keep warm at an altitude of ten thousand feet or higher when there's little oxygen to burn? You also wouldn't want to draw attention to your whereabouts.

Faint buzzers went off in Joe's head about Harold and Lexi's knowledge of and interest in Mansa Musa. Perhaps they were just brilliant people with a tremendous power of recall, but they sure knew a lot of details about the king and everything related to him. He thought it was odd that Harold, a man of the arts and history, knew all these details about moving and hiding large quantities of gold.

Or at least, that's what Harold admitted to. He hoped Joe would unveil a key piece of the puzzle that had eluded everyone for centuries. There was much to think about, but sleep began to call. Before he could go to sleep, however, he had to address a visitor.

JOE'S PAST

On occasion, Joe would be visited at night by an old acquaintance, his past. Using the word "friend" wouldn't be an accurate or fair description. It was a frequent visit but not always a nice one; usually it went poorly. His weren't the normal fears and frustrations most people experience. Too often, for too many years in too many tents or caves or wherever Joe was, at the end of the day with a bottle of beer or something stronger in hand, Joe would ponder *how the hell did I get here?* It wasn't that Joe would get rip-roaring drunk, as his rigid training wouldn't allow that. He would get awfully quiet and withdrawn though, even if he were around other people. He had done things that as a civilian seemed barbaric but in the broader context of national security made all the sense in the world. He could explain away those things.

The worst nights would be when he was all alone and would pull out a worn photo of himself with his Sudanese fiancé, and cry. Revenge had been swift, but certainly not sweet. Lexi had gone a long way toward filling the void and ending the pain, but something was still missing. He realized it was the joy and innocence of first love.

On those nights, his friend would often arrive with music, driving the mood even darker. It could be a song like *Cherish* by the Association that would drive more tears or *Help Me Girl* by the Animals, which would agitate him further.

The "how" was more than the literal, physical placement, and more like a "why." It was the how did a kid from Syracuse, New York and a 'plain vanilla' middle-class upbringing, wind up as a very highly trained near robotic intellectual machine for the U.S. government? What began as a three to five-year commitment, for one reason or another kept getting extended until he had finally had enough. Too many holidays, birthdays, and other celebrations were spent in locations devoid of color, absent of joy, absent of love in a clandestine surrounding all to improve the standing of the world. All too often, he had to stand by and accept situations he absolutely opposed and found appalling but couldn't change in any way. He had become scarred and inert, with little feeling.

This wasn't the way he was raised, which was to be like his father and home every night by five o'clock for the dinner his mom would make for their family of four. His dad was a career utility worker whose every day was predictable. Ditto with his mom, who worked part-time in a school cafeteria. Everything was predictable and secure. It was the law of unintended consequences that led him to his first interesting and good-paying job with a government agency, which led him overseas, which led to longer periods of silence, which led him here, tonight, drinking a cold beer, alone, and wondering what happened to the small house with a white picket fence, a few kids, and a loving stay-at-home wife?

He often wondered what was missing in his character that drove him to these foreign assignments. What was he denying? As far as he knew, no one on either side of his family had this kind of wanderlust in them. He wondered if he could commit to this ideal lifestyle. The few desk jobs he had suffered through bored him. He wasn't a paper-pusher.

The bigger issue was could he ever love again, or was he so badly scarred from what had happened in the Sudan that he could never completely open up and release his true self to another woman or children? It had already been a long time. He was also getting old and soon would be the same age his dad was when he was born. He loved his dad and mom very much and had a great upbringing, but it was different being a dad in your forties than in your twenties.

The answer for so many years had been "not you," but now as a private citizen, there was hope things were changing. His nights now were in a nice seventh-floor apartment, a situation far more comfortable than he had been used to for most of his adult life. He had a gorgeous girlfriend. When he was being evaluated while at Dartmouth for selection into the elite government services he eventually was chosen for, it was known from the beginning that he was scholastically superior as well as for having the mental and physical stamina of long-distance runners and those who participated in college rowing. What still had to be determined was his ability to deal with the environmental realities of the third world. He had passed that test with flying colors years ago.

Now the challenge was to peacefully transition from a CIA "persona" to that of as private citizen. His new world in Cambridge had neither flies nor the constant smell of death. Air conditioning took care of the gripping heat and humidity that few Americans experience nowadays for more than a few hours at a time, and usually by choice at a beach or a pool.

At the other extreme was the heat and dryness of the mountain deserts, conditions that dried one's throat and eyes in a matter of days. Nowadays, hot and cold water were always available at the turn of a faucet. No more daily struggle for survival amidst the sounds, sights, and outright cries of the region's impoverished. What Joe had now was what most people in the world strived for and would be happy with.

What he desperately needed however, was a life.

FIVE

The King's Journal

It was bitterly cold that January evening when Delta
Airlines flight #58 took off from Boston's Logan airport
bound for Paris' Charles de Gaulle airport. Joe had taken
Harold's advice regarding additional source material and
had received Skip's approval for a trip to Paris. Joe's Boston
attire served him well there where the snow had been
exchanged for an uncomfortable and cold dampness.
Welcome to the continent!

His first day in Paris was spent trying to adjust to the
six-hour time difference. Even seasoned travel professionals
found it difficult. He did review his plan to visit key government agencies including the French Foreign Legion, The
French Geographic Society, The Arab Institute and the
GDSE, France's external intelligence agency.

There were documents at both the French Foreign
Legion and the GDSE describing skirmishes with local
North African tribes, but the majority of these were of
recent history dating from France's involvement in the

region and primarily separatist groups and not religious. There was some discussion on the difficulties living in the region, but Joe knew that firsthand. The current information the GDSE gave him regarding the various tribes in the region and the degree of political stability was valuable.

While reviewing some project material at one of these agencies, it was suggested he visit the Musee d'Arabe. There he found an old translation into French of Mansa Musa's pilgrimage to Mecca. It documented much of what Lexi and Harold had told him. His pilgrimage took him through Mali, Algeria, Niger, Chad, Sudan, Egypt and, Saudi Arabia. This was all done through the dry highlands of these countries, not the deserts or jungles.

It confirmed that, Musa brought and gave away so much gold, he disrupted the economies for more than ten years because of the gold inflation. He tried to rectify things by buying back as much as he could. Joe wondered where it went.

He also found other writings that spoke of the king's fortune, but in Arabic. Part of his training was to become fluent in several languages, including Arabic. These journals discussed the disappearance of the king's fortune, variably describing and exaggerating what was likely an even larger fortune when all was accounted for. Other writings described the visit of Musa's predecessor to what was now believed to be the Canary Islands and his disappearance there. Sometime after returning to Mali from his pilgrimage to Mecca, Musa sent a large party to the Canary Islands to look for his predecessor, but with no luck. Chasing down a rumor of his being seen in what is now Cameroon, he sent a similar expedition there. No luck as well. Joe thought it odd that he would send armies so far away to chase down rumors. What did these countries share? What were these men chasing?

The king's journal described the later years of his rule and his concern for his vast wealth, and how to safely protect it. These descriptions appeared to be in code or riddles, with a great deal of period embellishment and storytelling. Joe couldn't make anything of it and thought it interesting that, as the timeline progressed, the messages became more cryptic. Perhaps he would learn more at a later time as it had been suggested by the Musee staff that he speak with a storyteller to learn more of the detailed history. Arrangements were made that day to meet with one the following afternoon, Mr. Aziz Booka. That evening, Joe mentally prepared his list of questions.

THE STORYTELLER

The region's history, mythologies, and oral traditions are passed down from generation to generation through storytellers. Each tribe has a different name for these people; the Tuareg call them agguta, while the Malinke call them griots. Although the oral history may have more than the usual amount of embellishing, it does do a good job of relating the facts and events of centuries past. France's involvement with Mali beginning in 1892 opened the door for a select few people to emigrate and as a result their availability in France.

While primarily relocating to southern France, some Africans did move to the Paris area, with its learning institutions and general wealth. Through the Arab Institute, Joe was introduced to Mr. Aziz Booka, a storyteller originally from Timbuktu. For a fee of fifty euros, Mr. Booka would answer your questions and tell "stories" for one hour. Mr. Booka lived in the Twentieth Arrondissement, one of the poorer districts of Paris with a large immigrant population.

It was safe to say that Mr. Booka was well into his seventies and five foot six inches tall. He was North African of Berber descent. He had fine features and brown coloring with deep lines in his face, indicating a slender build underneath the customary robes he wore that day. On his head was the traditional kufi, a brimless short and round cap that storytellers were wont to wear. Horrible teeth could have been due to a poor diet, hygiene, smoking, or any combination of the three. The robes and hat were faded white in color. A milky left eye was an indication of an untreated cataract. Large conservative glasses completed the "look."

"Mr. Booka, what a pleasure meeting you," said Joe in French with a smile on his face and an outreached hand. "I have so much to learn about your country and people, and at least today, only one hour to learn it. I'm wondering what you can tell me about Mansa Musa."

"The pleasure is mine. Ah, the king was a very good one to the people and extremely wise. Wise enough to know that knowledge, special knowledge, was possessed by others. It was King Abubakari who created the circumstances for Musa's anointment. The king and those before him brought wise men to the kingdom that could read the stars at night and learn so much. They knew by watching the curved movement of the stars at night and the changing winds from the sea that the world wasn't square or flat and was much bigger than the eye could see.

The king sent a large expedition off to the northwest by sea to explore the real boundaries of the world. When they didn't return after two years, he decided to mount his own, even larger expedition, putting Musa in charge with the decree that if he didn't return, Musa would continue, as the lawful king. The king never returned to the kingdom and as decreed, Musa assumed the throne."

"What did Musa do with his time? What was his legacy?"

"Musa was a man of knowledge and deep religion. As "Mansa," he was also the connection between the living and their ancestral spirits. He brought in many additional wise men who were experts in metals, architecture, mathematics, medicine, languages, and other specialties, even more so after his return from Mecca. His wealth at that time was extraordinary, and he brought scholars and scribes and established the world's second greatest university at Sankore. He had thousands of scribes prepare one million documents. Imagine that, one million! The book people were ever so important."

"He had great wealth. It was obvious and attractive to everyone as well. How did he protect it?" pressed Joe.

"He protected it with the stars, the sun and the children of Dilla." Booka placed emphasis on the word "Dilla" by exhaling strongly when speaking it. His breath was industrial strength, and Joe hoped his facial expression didn't evidence any reaction.

"What did the stars have to do with it?" asked Joe.

"You needed the stars to guide you," was the reply.

"And the sun?"

"To light the way."

"By Dilla, do you mean the town in Ethiopia?" questioned a surprised Joe. He knew of Dilla from his travels.

"Yes. Originally they were all from Dilla. Not all eventually were from Dilla, but subsequent breeding led to them being called that name."

"What do you mean 'breeding'? Why would you breed children?" asked Joe with a quizzical look on his face.

"The children were special. They were all from halfway to the sky, so they could run very far and fast if the Mansa required it." Mr. Booka emphasized this by waving his arm in a sweeping arch. "They were fed special foods and drinks, so they could see and hear and do special things. It's said they could see the sun and hear whispers in the wind. They were also Christians and kept separate from other children."

"I hear you, sir, but what did they do for Musa? Why did they have to run so far? What do you mean 'see the sun'? We all can see the sun. If you look straight into it, you'll burn your eyes out. What do you mean by 'whispers in the wind'? What were they looking for or listening to? There has to be more to this. What were they protecting?"

"They were protecting his wealth and the Book of Secrets."

"Tell me more about the Book of Secrets," queried Joe.

"It was a special book that only Musa or his most important court members could see. It contained the knowledge of all of Musa's great wealth and the secrets of conversing with the spirits of the ancestors.

"Were the Dilla people only boys? Did they have sisters?"

"Their sisters were raised to be the wife of the other boys and to maintain the dedication and purity of the breed."

"What happened when Musa died?"

"His death started a very dark period when life became cheap and order disappeared," said Booka. "Many were persecuted in trying to find the book, but the book people and the children protected it. No one ever found it. The wealth disappeared from the face of the earth, passing back to the ancestors, for now."

The questions and discussion continued throughout the contracted time, after which Mr. Booka abruptly said, "Your hour is up, my son, and I've got to go. It was nice to meet you." Joe left that afternoon, trying to put the pieces together. He couldn't ask questions fast enough and promised Mr. Booka to return soon.

THE SECRET CHURCH

In his review of obscure documents on Mansa Musa in the Musee D'Aribe in Paris, Joe came across an account in Arabic of Musa's court. Although he was a Muslim, he couldn't ignore the religions and beliefs that had existed in his empire for hundreds of years, especially when it was to his advantage. While Mali was a monarchy ruled by the Mansa (or Master), much of the state was in the hands of court officials. This meant the empire could survive periods of instability. The empire was also culturally diverse, being multi-cultural and multi-linguistic. While primarily Islamic, the kingdom accommodated local Christian and Jewish religious groups. The Mansa wasn't only the head of state but also a religious leader, with a direct link to the spirits of the land and guardian of the ancestors.

Another document described the existence of a little known or secret sect called the Order of the Gazelle. Harold had referred to it months earlier. They maintained a low-key presence for Christians in his kingdom. While Musa didn't always agree with them, he did realize they possessed a fervor and inner strength that could be counted on. After realizing he had to correct the problem he had created by giving away billions of dollars' worth of gold and other treasures, he also had to address the problem of growing conflict within his kingdom.

Various groups and regions fought for recognition and obviously the spoils that went with it. With a total kingdom value in excess of five hundred billion dollars, and weak and quarreling heirs adding to the problem, Musa realized he needed to provide for safekeeping of his kingdom's wealth until the proper time. This meant hiding the one billion dollars in gold he returned with from Mecca, but also the balance of the wealth. He needed people, processes, and locations that would provide the maximum of security.

The church provided for many of the people. All

members were Christians, and philosophically against slavery and pro-women. They had been in his kingdom prior to his hajj. They became involved in the mission as soon as his entourage crossed the Red Sea into Africa. Joe wondered if the church still existed or had faded away over the centuries. He would bring this up when he met again with Mr. Booka.

STORY II

Two days later, Joe went back to the storyteller for another visit, or more appropriately "session." This time, he paid for two hours of stories.

"Good day, Mr. Booka." Joe smiled. "I've been thinking about what you told me the other day and have additional questions. I hope you can help me understand more about your people."

"Good day to you, my son. Ask your questions, and I'll do my best." Booka looked like he was wearing the exact same clothes he had on two days earlier. He poured both small cups of fresh coffee.

"In our last meeting, you mentioned all the brilliant people Musa brought to his kingdom and staff. Among them you mentioned the 'book people.' What book are you talking about?"

Booka slightly smiled and almost chuckled when he replied, "The people of the book are the Yahoodees." Joe had a puzzled look on his face. "The Yahoodees are the Jews. The Muslims called the Yahoodees or Jews the 'Book

People' because they read from the Torah. The book people were extremely important. They were among the brightest and most important members of the king's court."

"Jews, in West Africa in the 1300s?" replied a surprised Joe.

"Don't look so surprised, my son. The Jews had dispersed throughout Africa much earlier than Musa's time. They were highly desirable members of many kings' staffs. The fact they were complete 'outsiders' and subject to quick and brutal reprisals if they cheated, stole, or lied made them trustworthy. They were brilliant people. He shared with them many important things, including the Book of Secrets."

Here we go again. Joe didn't know how to react to that one. He had heard that name for the first time at the previous session and wondered if he was being played, either with bullshit or efforts to keep him coming back for more at fifty euros per hour. If this was important information, he didn't like it being parsed out.

"Can you tell me more about the Book of Secrets?"

"The book was a collection of critical items. With whom did they have treaties, from whom did they receive tax money? How much is in the treasury, what is in the treasury, who controls it? Remember all wealth does not glitter! Who are the key civilian and military leaders? Where has the king stored his wealth and who guards it and most importantly, how to get to it? In addition, only the king and the chief trusted book person knew who had the keys."

Joe, again a little suspicious, asked, "What were the keys?"

"According to legend, there were seven keys required to access the Book of Secrets and then the king's fortune. Only he knew what they were and who had them. The chief knew who had them but not what they were or did. For example, one of the keys could be a key that you put in a lock. Another key could be verbal directive like, at high noon, the sun will shine on a specific number and at six p.m., it shines on another. Follow that sequence to open the lock. There could also be false keys to throw his enemies off and into a different direction."

Joe was a little more interested as well as confused and asked, "What happened to the keys? Have they been found? If not, how many are still out there?'

"This is what people have been looking for the last seven hundred years. This was Mansa's way of protecting his wealth in case of revolt or invasion. No one knows where they are or what they are or even if they still exist. The final key, however, would be delivered from the blue sky above and would be a bright and pure light, guiding the faithful to the treasures they had guarded for so many years." While saying this, Booka positioned his arms as if he were personally guiding the light from above to the table in front of them.

How prosaic, Joe thought. "What do you mean by a 'bright and pure light from the blue sky above?' Many cultures have references to a blinding bright light either delivering someone or something to or removing it from the earth. What is different about this light; who will see it?"

"The faithful will see it," said Booka, with conviction in his voice. "I can't tell you any more about the meaning of the light. I can guess (chuckling), however, they weren't referring to a laser." That got a lame smile from Joe.

"So, what happened?"

"Well, the king died supposedly without telling anyone his secrets. There was a struggle within the king's family over who would succeed him and just as important, the chief book person disappeared."

"Killed?"

"No, disappeared, to reappear at a future date, when God so dictates."

"Killed?" said Joe in a firm and slow low tone.

"Perhaps," replied Booka, with a slight shrug of his shoulders and display of his palms. He reached for the pot of coffee, pouring a fresh cup for himself and Joe. After taking a small sip of this hot potion, Joe continued with his questions.

"The last time I was here you told me that Musa protected his wealth with the stars, the sun, and the children of Dilla. How do they all fit in?"

"Okay, they had a mantra that was something like, 'The sun, moon, and stars with the nourishment of water and earth will guide the children to the key that unlocks the door of reward.' Booka loosely waved his arms in an animated fashion while saying this. "Remember there could be a translation issue after all these years. Yes, the stars are one of the keys, as is the sun. I don't know exactly what this all means. They point to some place or to a name. The legend refers to the riches that lie between the skies above and the good earth below. The Children of Dilla, however, were ultimately bred to serve as the king's loyal guards."

Joe had to challenge this comment and questioned, "How could children matchup against trained adult warriors who would be much larger than them and could be fitted with horrible weapons?"

"I don't know, my son, but it may be a case of brains over brawn or something close."

"Do you know what they looked like?"

"They were unlike most Ethiopians which among Africans are considered quite attractive people. They were physically small with long heads and long ears and odd-looking eyes! They weren't as dark skinned as most Ethiopians either. Wait a minute." Booka called for an aide and gave instructions in Arabic to fetch something. "Ah, here we go." The aide had returned with a pile of old papers and, through his good eye, Booka went through them until he found what he was looking for. "Here is an old illustration," and he turned to show it to Joe. Joe hoped his eye reflexes didn't give away too much, because the drawing was of a tiger child.

"What happened to the children of Dilla? Do they still exist?"

"I imagine they do since the king's fortune hasn't been discovered yet."

"How do you know the fortune hasn't been discovered yet?"

"I'm assuming that because it was so huge, trying to spend it would be immediately noticed." Joe thought, *good point, maybe.*

"Who are the tiger children?"

"I don't know, never heard of them."

"But they supposedly lived in this area too."

"My son, there are no tigers in Africa. They are an Asian cat. Maybe you're thinking about India?" Booka was right and Joe should've known better. He made a mental note to talk to Sanjib about this when he arrived home. Maybe the "tigers" and children of Dilla were one in the same. It was time to return to the main topic.

"Okay, if the children of Dilla are still around, who is 'breeding' them and paying them and their expenses?"

"Most but not all of the king's money was deeply hidden. There's money in various places in the world to continue the guard until the fortune can be revealed. There's some money available that answers some of the prayers of the poor."

"And when will the 'door of reward' be opened?" asked Joe.

"When the rightful heir comes forward to lead the king's people," proclaimed Booka, slightly slapping his open hand on the table.

It had now been an hour and a half, and the storyteller was getting a little tired, but Joe pressed on, fully intending to use his two hours of time.

"What can you tell me about the Order of the Gazelle?" asked Joe with a measured meter to his words. It was a slight delay, but a delay nonetheless, that Joe picked up on in Mr. Booka's reply. If a word balloon could have expressed Mr. Booka's silent thoughts, it would have said, 'You've done your homework, my son.'

"The Order of the Gazelle was the secret name given to

the Christian sect that worked for the king. They were loyal and trustworthy."

"How and why did they pick that name?"

"Well, gazelles are a local animal and known to be fast and agile."

"Could the children of Dilla been members of this sect?"

"Quite possibly, but as junior members, and not in leadership positions. Remember they were from far away and relatively young."

"Does the church still exist?"

"That's possible too, but you would need to visit Timbuktu to verify that. If it exists, it would be there."

His two hours were just about up, and Joe had run out of questions, for now. He thanked Mr. Booka and bade him adieu.

Joe had to think clearly about what he had been told in his two sessions with the storyteller and resist the urge to make decisions based solely on today's thinking. Booka knew a lot about Musa so it must be a popular topic in their culture. He had to keep in mind that Booka was a storyteller and entertainer and, to him, the plain truth wouldn't get in the way of a good and prosperous story. He would have to find another storyteller to corroborate what he had just heard. Before he did that, he would need to do much more homework on the topic and then create specific questions to gaps in the narrative.

He also had to accept that if Booka was correct in saying that money has been available all these years to continue the guard, then Booka, too, was probably on the payroll and filing reports on Joe's visits to someone with a checkbook.

Key things had to be correctly assessed, as confusing as some of them were. Booka's answers were all over the place, riddles in response to direct questions. For Joe to do this, he had to go back to his training and list them in his head;

1. The seven keys aren't likely to be door keys as we know them, be they metal, plastic pass cards, or fobs. They could be mental or physical challenges like "keys to success in business" or "how to run a marathon." They could be abstract references to other things. It's possible there are one or two physical keys required to open a vault or safe like a safety deposit box in a bank vault. How and where do you find the first key? Today, no one knows.

2. "A pure light" is used too often in ancient folklore but with a bright shining beam coming down to earth. This interpretation is too difficult to fathom in today's world. The reference to a light and the earth are reasonable points of any story. The "pure" light needs to be deciphered. Is the earth the ground, or is it referring to something else?

3. The number seven is an often-used number in nursery rhymes. It's considered a lucky number in several major cultures. The people living in this region were much affected by the sun and the stars. Several celestial objects including the Little Dipper with seven stars could be clearly

seen in the regions clear desert skies. Was it a reference to a celestial map?

4. Joe will have to investigate the children of Dilla as soon as possible. Their being bred had nothing to do with being trustworthy and loyal and more to do with physical characteristics of some kind that gave the children unusual sensual abilities separate from physical conditioning.

5. It seems incredible that funds and an organization to manage them have been secretly in place for seven hundred years!

6. Does the Order of the Gazelle still exist, and where?

7. Several days ago, Mr. Booka mentioned that the children of Dilla were fed special food and water so they could see the sun and hear the wind. That needs to be deciphered because today, he mentioned cat-like eyes. So, it is safe to say they had unusual vision enhanced by something they ate and/or drank. So, what else could they see, or could they see better like high altitude eagles and hawks?

8. He should have pursued Booka's comment that all wealth does not glitter. It's referring to something other than gold; it could be salt or books or forms of knowledge.

The general hypothesis was coming together, however:

The gold and other valuables were hidden at high altitudes along and adjacent to the Sahel where only special people could handle the harsh conditions. These would likely be the children of Dilla or members of the Order of the Gazelle. Their enhanced senses and a special light would somehow lead to the gold. It was time to put together a plan and get ready to act.

There was still in existence an organization of some global means waiting to get its hands on the gold and other valuables when their locations were revealed. At this time, its size and strength couldn't be determined.

That last evening, he took the Metro to the Trocadero station and crossed the street to gaze at the Eiffel Tower for ten to fifteen minutes. One couldn't go to Paris without making this little inspirational side trip, preferably with arms around a lover. After this, he ate dinner alone at one of the cafes adjacent to The Metro station. The next day, he caught a mid-day flight home, with a lot to interpret, assess, and take action on.

SIX

Mount Wachusett

It was time to test a few hypotheses in a scenario (high altitude, remote, rocky, clear air) as close to the north African region as possible. To do that, Joe called his friend, Matt.

"Top of the morning to you, Matt," said Joe. "How are you doing?"

"Hey Joe," exclaimed Matt. "I'm okay. To what do I owe this pleasure?"

"A quick question; how good are your sensors?"

"Best in the world," was his short and simple answer.

"Great. I need a favor. I need to test that capability. I have several signals I want you to read."

"Okay but keep in mind that being located near a metro area or a military base could overpower your signal," warned his friend.

"I understand. Here is what I'm going to do. I'll set up several test letters on a local mountaintop outside of Boston. There should be no interference at all. Figure the letters to be six feet in length and eight inches in width that will receive a UV signal and glow. I'm also going to bury several metals to see if you can find and identify them and include several "bonus" signals for you to read. I'll give you the general coordinates, date, and time, and you tell me what you see. Will you need to reposition any satellites?"

"Nope, Massachusetts is always covered; a lot of spies there. Just tell me where and when."

"Sounds good... Should be fun! I'll call you with the date!"

Joe knew from his training that some woods like Black Locust would glow under an ultraviolet light. Appraisers of rare wooden furniture would usually shine a powerful UV flashlight on the various surfaces of a piece of furniture to authenticate it. Certain rare woods glowed while close copies didn't. He wanted this to be a true test of the NSA's satellite sensor skills, and confirmation of the technology Musa's people might have used seven hundred years ago to send secret messages.

He bought two one-hundred-gallon fish tanks to create a small waterfall through which he could shine several high-powered portable spotlights. The balance of the test required a portable pump and a couple of hoses, two gallons of gasoline, two old cell phones, and five cases of beer. For the metals test, they brought six by six-inch pieces of gold-plated steel and silver-plated steel. A large plastic bag of topsoil to cover the metals was purchased at a local garden shop. Everything would be loaded into a nondescript Ford model 150 pickup truck.

Joe needed help to pull this off and took a chance by asking Sanjib and Kevin. Joe told them the test was a part of their program, and it and its results must remain a secret from everyone, including Skip until the data could be correlated, evaluated, and documented. They promised their cooperation and silence. As an extra precaution, they wore sunglasses and ski masks through the gate and covered the license plates and inspection sticker with duct tape, should there be cameras at the gate or the top.

The test would be on the rocky top of Mount Wachusett, over two thousand feet high and fifty miles northwest of Boston, and nowhere near an active military site. They were lucky that snowfall that winter to date had been minimal. That evening, they picked the lock that closed the road to the summit and drove the three miles to the top, relying on the light of the full moon to guide their way. They loosely put the lock in place for their return. They alarmed it to let them know if anyone followed them.

What a view! The February night was crystal clear, with a one-hundred-mile perspective. A nearby koi fish pond would supply the needed water without causing suspicion. The test would be for fifteen minutes only. The date coincided with a local college's homecoming weekend, and Joe chose the letters of a local fraternity XT to further throw off attention. Some of these fraternities had a history of pulling stunts, and this would be a good one. This mountain is adjacent to the approach route for planes flying into Boston from the west and southwest. With the chances high that an oncoming plane or two might report the test, Joe wanted it to appear to be a fraternity prank.

Boston's skyline lit up the sky to the east. To the north, west, and south, there was nothing but darkness, with an occasional flickering light from a far-off town. They were there by nine p.m. for the ten-p.m. test. Setting up the letters was easy. The difficult part was setting up and adjusting the water tank so that it would allow just enough water to fall to create a thin lens four feet wide through which they could shine the spotlights and hopefully refract UV light on the letters.

Joe had decided to make two bonus tests without telling Matt what they were. Earlier in the day, he collected a large trash bag full of fungi he had cut off various tree stumps in the woods. Off to the side and out of the range of the agreed-upon tests, he made a five-foot diameter "O" out of the fungi.

Joe also made a crude UV transmitter at home. It was a five-gallon bucket that had a 12-volt black light placed in the bottom and positioned so that it shone up and out. Over the lip of the bucket, he placed several filters intended to remove as much of the black light that people could see. The top filter had an eight inch by eight inch capital "M" printed on it and just below in a space of two inches high by four inches wide were the letters ATT. Joe hoped Matt would comment on these side tests. At ten o'clock, they were ready to roll.

They had Matt on a cell phone, and he read the mountaintop. After five minutes of trying, he couldn't read any of the wooden letters. They started the water pump and began the waterfall. Two million candlepower spotlights shone through the water and as expected, refracted the light into a spectrum. With an aperture made from a cardboard box, everything went as hoped. And there they had it, giant glowing golden letters in the clear February sky, courtesy of the filtered infrared light coming from the fish tank and shining on the Black Locust planks. They were impressed, as were the pilots of United Airlines flight #123 now approaching Boston's Logan airport from Chicago.

Within five minutes, word came back from Matt that we had a six foot by eight inch X and a six foot by eight inch T. He also said that while we didn't ask the question, the wood was Black Locust, and who made the "O?" He thought the UV "Matt" was poor engineer's humor. The metals were detected as small and low-quality pieces of gold and silver. This was test one, courtesy of U.S. government spy satellites. Low-flying drones could do an even better job.

Test two was a hypothesis on the level of the technology Musa had seven hundred years ago which could have used either flowing water and an aperture cut in a leather hide or a crystal prism to separate the components of the visible light spectrum to isolate the ultraviolet portion. It was the UV portion of the light that caused chemicals in the wood to glow or fluoresce. The same basic setup could have been used to identify hidden treasures or give otherwise secret directions.

Test three showed that a satellite, drone, or some young people could see what people with normal vision couldn't, the name "Matt" outlined in a whitish blue color. Test four was just to satisfy Joe's curiosity. Many common fungi glowed in the dark but in the past, the glow was only detectable with a ten-minute exposure. It was another form of signaling used in covert operations. Obviously, detection capabilities had improved tremendously in recent years.

With the tests finished, the pump was shut off, and the wood was stacked in bonfire fashion. Gasoline was poured over everything, the cellphones activated and quickly placed under the wood, and they were off. An automatic sparking device was also left behind as additional insurance. Ten minutes later, the call was made to a now-working cell phone, and the sky lit up. What an explosion and fire! When American Airlines flight #32 made the same approach ten minutes later and saw the burning letters and fire, Joe and his guys were already off the mountain and on the interstate highway, heading home. Joe initially felt sorry for the fraternity but then thought they wouldn't be persecuted because there would be no evidence. On the plus side, the notoriety would be huge and worth the initial aggravation.

KARAOKE

March was an ugly time of year in Boston. Winter's fiercest months were in the past having been replaced with rain, slush, and mud. Five months of trash would soon re-appear from the melting snow drifts, as would deep and dangerous potholes in the streets. Over the past few months, Joe and Lexi had begun seriously dating. Lexi invited Joe to join her and some of her co-workers for drinks at Murphy's, on karaoke night. Joe's work buddies also showed up and were joined by Sanjib's brother, Ravi and his wife, Nara, who had been convinced it would be a fun time. Two tiger children were also there that night, a fact not lost on Sanjib.

Karaoke night was a hoot. Performers from the audience had a choice of props to use during their singing. Hats, a guitar, and sports equipment were there, as well as a surfboard and a motor scooter. That night, most people were feeling good and a little drunk. While Sanjib and Kevin were perfectly comfortable in this setting, Ravi looked like a fish out of water. Nara was uncomfortable in a raucous bar scene like this as well.

Sanjib pointed out the two tiger children to his brother, who also shared bad memories of them.

Feeling no pain, Joe sang along with many of those performing on stage from his seat in the audience. He was egged on to sing by Lexi's friends and agreed to it if Lexi joined him. After a little prodding, she grabbed his hand, and they bounced on stage.

As with most karaoke scenes, the songs were all over the place, reflecting the likes of the singers. The crowd at Murphy's had just suffered through renditions of "My Way" and "Mame," and Joe decided to shake things up a bit. Joe's song that evening was "Scatman," a tongue twister if there ever was one, written and performed by American singer Scatman John. It was about his difficulties in overcoming stuttering. In time, it became an international dance hit and a stable of high-level karaoke contests. After an initial look of horror at Joe's verbal stumbling, Lexi laughed as did the crowd. This was a side of Joe that no one had seen before. He was a performer!

At this point, the brothers decided to go over and introduce themselves to their two African compadres who had now come together and were chatting. Ravi started the conversation, figuring he would be the more civil of the brothers.

"Hi boys, long way to go for a beer, isn't it?" ask Ravi.

"Not really, maybe two or three miles," tiger child #1 replied. "We live just down the road."

"Wow, I would have sworn you were from the Sudan or Chad, you know, the high-altitude guys that defended their ancestors' spirits! You look familiar." Ravi wasn't backing down.

"I don't know what you're talking about. My parents moved here a long time ago, before I was born actually. I'm an American. How about you?" He turned to the other one without saying his name.

The second tiger child was the one Sanjib met during an earlier visit to this bar. He was not putting up as convincing a front as his counterpart, remembering Sanjib's more direct conversation.

"The same with me," was his feeble reply.

"Wow, you could have fooled me," chirped Sanjib. You guys look just like the characters we would see in the villages, dancing around and harassing foreigners like us." At this point, Sanjib broke into a silly dance to mimic what he and Ravi remembered from Africa.

At this exact time, Joe and Lexi were taking their bows to an appreciative and noisy crowd, led by Lexi's work team. Someone in Lexi's group yelled out, "akazoo chella," which Lexi loudly repeated, laughing and pointing an outstretched finger to the sky. Sanjib and Ravi caught it right away as being one of the phrases the tiger children used. The two tiger children also caught it and made the mistake of looking at Ravi and Sanjib in the eyes. At this point, all four knew exactly what had happened. The stories Ravi and Sanjib had just been told weren't convincing.

"Sorry for the mistake. Have a good evening," said Ravi. With that, he and Sanjib went back to the bar and joined Nara and Kevin.

Later in the evening, Lexi and her group left, and Joe joined his work group in front of the bar to have another beer. He heard Sanjib and Ravi discussing their recently ended encounter. At this point, Joe was interested.

Joe asked the brothers, "Guys, do you remember exactly where these events happened... I mean the city or towns?" Both mentioned different villages, in different countries. Joe recognized both as being in the foothills of high mountains. At this point, Kevin interrupted the conversation and while slightly tipping his beer in Joe's direction, asked the group, "What do you think of our buddy's performance tonight?"

"Outside of the insult at the end, very entertaining," stated Nara.

"What do you mean?"

"Well, Lexi's comment at the end was a bit crude," replied Ravi.

At the end of the evening, when everyone was leaving, it was raining hard and foggy. Ravi had Nara wait at the door while he went to get their car. Joe and Sanjib had arrived there early in the evening and found parking spots in the adjacent parking lot. Ravi had been forced to find a parking space way down the road on the main boulevard that ran in front of the bar. Sanjib offered him a ride to his car, but Ravi waved him off and took off down the street alone.

There were snow drifts to the side of the road with deep slush, now super-saturated by the evening's rain. In retrieving the car, Ravi was forced for some distance to walk in the street, watching where he was walking and dealing with cars and trucks approaching him from the rear and splashing thin sheets of slush on him repeatedly. He had just reached his car and, without looking back at the oncoming traffic, opened the door to get in, first knocking the slush off his right shoe before doing so. That five to six-second delay was the difference between life and death. He was hit and killed instantly by a hit-and-run driver. He and the door lay in the street in the driving rain while onlookers called for an ambulance and desperately tried to save his life.

While waiting at the door for Ravi's return, Nara heard the ever-strengthening sirens of the approaching ambulances, ignoring their meaning until the flashing lights and screaming people made it painfully obvious. She ran down the now-blocked street and in the rain, cradled Ravi's head in her lap amid the cacophony of lights, sounds, and the elements surrounding her. Her life had changed forever.

According to Hinduism, when the physical body dies, the individual soul has no beginning and no end. It may pass to another through reincarnation, depending on one's karma. Those of the Hindu faith prefer to die at home surrounded by their family who will keep vigil. According to custom, the body remains at the home until it is cremated, which is usually within twenty-four hours after death. The ashes are typically scattered at a sacred body of water or at some other place of importance to the deceased. Per the request of his family, Ravi's ashes would be returned to India, where his parents and extended family would conduct a memorial service prior to interment.

The wake was held at Ravi and Nara's home in Arlington. All Sanjib's team as well as Skip's staff were in attendance. Also attending were work associates of Ravi and Nara and other friends and neighbors. Sanjib said in a very distressed voice, "It's all my fault. We should have insisted he take a ride from us from the bar." Mah tried consoling him without any luck.

Joe tried to console Nara, who was even more alone in America than before. He fumbled for words that would provide some level of comfort with no luck. Nara would give him empty but stoic looks. Joe struggled with this event in the days and weeks that followed. In another place at another time, this would have been a planned "hit," as was commonplace in third-world countries. His CIA self said "hit," but the new private citizen wanted to believe in fate. Why would anyone want to kill a chemical engineer?

NEXT MONTHLY REVIEW

Skip called the next monthly meeting to order. Thirteen months into the program and problems were starting to appear.

"Okay, folks, let's go. Joe, what's new?"

"I made a trip earlier in the month to D.C. to meet again

with people in the NSA departments. We discussed sensor improvements. They are making tremendous progress in several areas, and hope we are too. Nothing major at this time to report on." Skip nodded to Sanjib.

"Okay, the team wrote twenty-five thousand lines of code last month, which was the highest level so far and on target. We just finished installing the latest software and chips. Speeds are ramping up. We're still debugging and hope to have things fully functional next week."

Skip was a bit annoyed with this statement and said, "Hold on there! What do you mean debugging? What the hell is going on? It appears all you're doing is constantly debugging?"

Sanjib was equally annoyed. "We're constantly debugging, matching new software requirements and codes with these hardware 'fantasy speeds' you have us now using. We're talking about military computer chips that are much more advanced than what was available just last year. What is it you're thinking of that needs 'shutter speeds of a gazillionth of a second?' High tech to these mountain and desert guys is a goat or a pickup truck!"

"People, we don't know where this project will take us, or others. Maybe it's only improved visual warnings, but it could be something else. It's possible our platform could be used with sensors still to be developed. Who knows?" Skip calmed down a bit and in a more relaxed tone, asked, "What are some of the problems you're having?"

"Recruitment remains an issue. Mildred, would you comment on this?"

"What Sanjib is saying is true. There's a lot of competition for experienced software writers, and it's difficult to match the offers they are getting from other companies in the region."

"Like what, Mildred?"

"Like flex time, long vacations, beer blasts, very generous health benefits, tuition reimbursement, and a relaxed work environment. We cannot match or even come close to what the large and liberal genetics research outfits are offering new employees, and we can't keep pushing our current employees the way we do. They won't put up with it. We may have to approach private companies and outsource some of our work. That will take time and be expensive."

Bob O'Neil interjected himself here quickly, "Historically, that will inflate the costs twenty to thirty percent."

"And it will add months or years to the project. It's not going to happen," stated Skip, matter of factly. "Bob and Mildred, let's meet separately and try to figure out a way to solve this problem. Kevin?"

"We're running into problems. We're doing as you instructed and pushing the equipment to the brink, no, make that destruction. We're getting good results but for some reason, as we increase the speed, we're losing the integrity of the wave shape and getting more display impurities on the computer screen. It changes with every test. We don't know the causes but are working on finding and fixing them. What began as dots has now progressed to lines, as if hair was getting into the focus area. It's like we 're looking at protozoa or something".

"We're questioning the quality of the power we're

receiving from the utility, as well as the quality of the power filters we're using. I'll let you know what we find out. One of the major problems with these high-speed computers is their high need for power to cool them down. We're running out of power and air-conditioning equipment, and it could be affecting our work."

"What the hell are you talking about? It's freezing out," yelled a now-impatient Skip.

"I'm talking about the need for super cooling of these components. Some of the large industrial supercomputers being built need the equivalent of their own industrial power plants for air conditioning. We're a tiny operation in a tiny building, and the place is getting hotter and hotter every day. We either dramatically upgrade the capacity of our laboratory air-conditioning system or cap our development efforts at pretty much where we are now, and sub-contract the work out to others."

Skip was uncharacteristically calm. He took a deep breath and said, "We're not going to lose our status or position in this R&D effort. Continue with your work. Kevin… you, Bob, and I need to meet on this to figure out our next steps. Hopefully, we can find the money and keep delays to a minimum. Kevin, please investigate what step improvements would bring us in performance. That will be a part of my pitch. Shit, I don't want to draw too much attention to changes outside the building with new power lines or transformers. I don't want a delay either."

"Skip, the area is being gentrified," said Joe. "Maybe part of your story could be that electric utility improvements are being made to handle the increasing needs of the neighborhoods." What Joe said was true. All of Cambridge and Somerville were undergoing continual gentrification. Chances are their building will be gone in five years and replaced with apartments.

"Good idea. It won't help us in the short term, but it may help get federal money. Okay, anything else? If not, meeting adjourned."

Kevin and Joe stopped into Sanjib's office as they moved down the hall. Kevin and Sanjib were annoyed. Kevin was the first to speak.

"This guy doesn't get it. We are paying top dollar for military-grade components. We shouldn't be having problems like this. It's like someone is messing with us, or we have forgotten to do something basic."

"He's probably never run an R&D project that was state-of-the-art software and hardware," added Sanjib.

The Future

Skip required all the team members to attend occasional seminars at the region's schools on a variety of topics that could influence the outcome of their project or that were good for general education. An additional benefit was that attendance was a general requirement of the program and most importantly from his perspective, it was billable time.

Recent discussions included topics on technical matters, modern art, and accounting. Joe became an active member of several women's rights groups as a result of attending one of their discussions. His first-hand knowledge of many of the key issues was much appreciated and valuable. He was being called on to speak about what he personally saw. The topic today was "God and the Future." Today's conference was being led by a male professor of philosophy at one of the region's universities and a female scientist for one of the city's biotech firms.

So began the male speaker, "Thank you all for joining us today on what we hope will be an interesting topic with interesting and thought-provoking discussions. Please approach this with an open mind. Let me begin by saying that the choice of the word "God" isn't meant to insinuate the Christian God or anyone's God. We're referring to the supreme being of each religion. We're not challenging the existence of the superior being in today's discussion."

Sanjib leaned over to Kevin and with a glare and whispered, "Hey, Kevin, isn't your God the almighty buck?"

Kevin whispered back, "So what? Shut up and pay attention."

The male speaker continued, "Over the centuries as more people around the world have been given a basic education, and as science has further developed, more and more things that had been described in various religions' holy books in fantasy ways to hype the story or get the point across to an uneducated audience have been either debunked or explained scientifically. For example, look at all the medieval and biblical references to giant, flying, flame-breathing dragons or sea monsters. Nope, they never existed. Other things like Moses parting of the Red Sea now have a rational technical explanation to them in lieu of, in Moses' case, the exaggerated giant waves of the movies.

"More things that were mysteries have now been rationally explained, but that doesn't diminish the fact that someone—God—still created the situation and helped us find the answer! Let's use medicine as an example. Witch doctors used to wave wands and chant and burn incense to cure diseases. Scientists can find cures for diseases with medicines. These medicines are complex chemical formulas, which are often extended mathematical equations. These formulas solve one problem after another and push them aside, but with the tools and empowerment given to us by... God, the creator of the universe."

The speaker went on, "Take genome mapping as another example. Over the centuries, people were described primarily by sex, color, surname, age, or basic looks. It is twenty-three pairs of genes that describe each one of us. These twenty-three pairs of genes comprise a formula that over time mankind will continue to develop a greater understanding of and will use this knowledge to further medical research and the health of all people. All of this is being done with tools given to us by "God.""

Joe listened closely. He wasn't sure where this guy was going. Some of this was going way over his head but the word "formula" caught his attention. After a few more comments, the male speaker said, "Okay, let's stop for a minute and take some questions."

Question number one came from a young woman sitting in the front of the audience, "As computer power increases over time, do you think we will move from the current alpha or alphanumeric ways of describing things to a purely numeric?"

The answer to her question was, "Maybe, but it will be a long time from now. A product name is understood by most people and commercially acceptable. It's also a lot shorter. For example, it's a lot easier to sell and/or prescribe 'Voldram, for fast relief of' than a string of numbers."

Question number two came from a male graduate student in the back of the hall, "How far can we take DNA research and evaluation?"

The answer came from the female scientist, who was somewhat laughing as she replied, "I'm not sure there is an answer. At this time, it's a moot issue. That's a lot of digits! Imagine taking twenty-three to the twenty-third power to describe someone instead of twenty-three pairs of alphanumeric characters. I think we looked at this one time. Twenty-three to the twenty third power is twenty million times a trillion trillion! It would take one heck of a computer. It's possible we will have one with that capability in fifty years. I expect we will continue to investigate the mystery of the genome, and at some point like we have with everything else, convert it into a pure numeric formula. I mean, every person in the USA has a unique social security number that describes only them. Why not the same with DNA?"

Let's go back to the tremendous number of digits and variations. What is it we are looking at; Purely human characteristics, or other species of plants and animals? Are some of the digits indicators of time? We don't know what's in there but with ever increasing frequency we are learning more and more. It's exciting!"

Her statement hit Joe like a lightning bolt. Developing

this computing capability wasn't fifty years away; it was three or five years. Military computer capabilities could be exceeding anyone's wildest imaginations by then. Computer calculations are now measured in units called petaflops, or one thousand trillion calculations per second. These monstrous systems are used by the militaries, pharmaceutical, and oil exploration companies to solve complex problems. Engineers are now working on the next generation of supercomputers that will use units of measure of exaflops, or one million trillion calculations per second.

"Time indicators, increasing frequency".

The rest of the Q and A didn't matter, and the discussion carried on after that for some time. Things were now clearer to Joe. There appeared to be order in the universe. Technology was already coding the world and human life. Every color, touch, emotion, taste, and smell could be described in a code. God had created a digital world, one in which every living creature was given a specific frequency for the afterlife, described by its unique DNA. Who knows what kind of "card file" he set up and whether it applied only to mammals, all animals, and plants, or even other planets?

It took millions of years for man to catch on to and catch up with his plans. The wait may be over, and soon.

The Revelation

After the discussion on God and the future, the team went back to Kevin's apartment and smoked some marijuana and talked about the presentation. Sanjib joked and told Joe and Kevin to think "cosmic" to get a better understanding of things. It had already hit Joe quickly, and his mind was racing...

As Pokey's computing speeds were getting much faster than anything previously known, the dots, lines and squiggles they were seeing could be snapshots of ever more sophisticated but still primitive life forms. Perhaps God had assigned every creature that ever lived a frequency of their own where their soul and visage resided for all time. Pokey's computers were currently at the low end of these frequencies, mistaking the very earliest forms of life on earth as "dust" on the screen. As time and technology moved on, the observed frequencies were increasing, and we moved on to more sophisticated organisms. Eventually, after who knew how many years, the frequencies would move into the human range.

In theory, in time, one may be able to dial in on one frequency, one person. One may be able to see and communicate with every person who had ever lived, ask any question.

Take it further. Every person had a different DNA. Suppose that DNA also included a code or was the code that indicated every person's frequency? Break the code and immediately approach that person for any of a thousand reasons. Maybe it's your mother, or George Washington, or Elvis. Do you want to torment Adolf Hitler? Maybe speak with Jesus directly, or a child. What if you had a serious disease and wanted to approach medical experts who had already passed on but could hopefully help you or a loved one?

It could get ugly quickly. The winner of this race could become the king of the world. How much do you think interested parties would pay to discredit competing politicians or governments or religions or philosophies? What would they pay to speak with military or technology experts of the past? What about social media giants who wanted access to every bit of information about every single person?

Already, genetic privacy had been compromised and would get worse as time marched on. People were discovering that their bloodlines weren't what they thought. The readily available DNA of a family member or cousin could be used against someone to solve a crime or if it indicated a risk of a future disease or debilitating mental state, or suicide. Being exposed as a third cousin of Jack the Ripper was something that few people would want to know or have exposed to the general public. The king's fortune was peanuts compared to the bigger topics that could be exposed and today, there was nothing that could be done to stop it.

The USA alone was worth in excess of one hundred trillion dollars. What was the world worth? Four hundred, five hundred trillion dollars? What was a couple of percent to keep the secrets of life intact? How about hourly rentals to speak with your ancestors or deceased loved ones? There would be no privacy for anything. Life might become even cheaper soon as today's technologies blossomed.

These were thoughts Joe decided not to share with his workmates that evening or anyone else thereafter. Some would think he was crazy while others would find this possibility chilling. Others, however, would think about how to capitalize on it. He found none of these options appealing at this time.

SEVEN

Sensor and Drone School

Joe, Skip, Sanjib, and Kevin were invited to and attended a two-day meeting at an obscure company located one hour from Palo Alto, California, to discuss and witness the advances in drones and sensor applications. The building bore the name of Vearil Innovations, which would be more likely to be mistaken for a supplier of trade show displays, or plastics in general, and not cutting-edge military weapons!

The main building itself was an old grayish-silver military hangar from the World War II era. The dry climate preserved it very well over the past seven decades. Its large volumetric dimensions lent itself well to demonstrating the equipment without external eyes seeing what was going on. Washington, D.C. management wanted the Pokey team leaders and others to have an idea of where the various programs were going and to impress upon them how important their contribution was to this key military effort.

Drone development had centered on reduced size,

increased capability, and lengthened flight time. The size reduction was on a trajectory that would introduce a fully functioning militarized hummingbird-sized drone in two years. Its duty would be recognizance and termination, with miniaturized weaponry on board. The miniaturized electronics on board were absolutely science fiction, as were the sensors. The sensor package was capable of hyperspectral imaging across the electromagnetic spectrum, enhanced facial recognition, gas recognition, and voice recognition. The wings were made of a material that also acted as a solar panel capable of recharging the on-board battery every two days. The drone was designed to be a "sleeper" in that it and possibly many others could be released from a larger and low-flying mother drone over an area of "interest" and be directed to the top of a telephone pole or monuments until needed. The maximum flying time was specified as thirty minutes.

In this scenario, a drone could be in a standby position waiting for an identified person of interest to leave a building to get into a car, for example, or to address a crowd from a podium. Armed and ready, it could go in for the kill. Another scenario would be the drone gaining entrance to a building and initiating a hunt for a specific person whose profile of speech, smell, or visual condition matched its proforma. Flying from room to room, the search could continue until the thirty-minute fly time was up. At that point, the drone operator would either enter a reset code to the drone, safely shutting it down and allowing the winged solar panels two days to recharge its battery or instruct it to self-destruct. Ground units could similarly release drones to target snipers. All data would be transmitted back to the mother drone or further to a satellite.

Another application could be using the drones for a mass attack on an enemy who was close but out of visual range. For example, twenty of these small attack drones could be released at once, preprogrammed to identify, hunt, and kill based on certain smells or heat maps, or even speech patterns. This would have been helpful in years past. The boys from Cambridge were impressed with what they saw. The message was delivered and understood. Project Pokey was important. They were pressed by a few people in attendance on when they would deliver their product. Their pat answer was on-time per the program requirements. They were in unison on the flight home. Any open positions needed to be filled ASAP.

WEEKENDS

Skip's adherence to a by-the-books forty-hour workweek (with ample overtime hours offered to all hardware engineers and required of the software writers) Monday through Friday, created an accommodating lifestyle for some. Joe and Lexi's relationship was able to flourish, particularly since neither had family in the region. They could spend a lot of time together in active and passive activities on the weekends, whether on day trips to the areas museums, bike paths along the North Shore, weekends on Cape Cod, or camping in the mountains.

Some of the time, they would spend at Joe's place along

the Charles River, but most of the time was spent at Lexi's apartment, closer to the action between Harvard and Kendall Squares. From Lexi's, they could walk everywhere or spend a quiet evening at home. Life was good.

One warm spring weekend, they rode bicycles along the ocean side up to Gloucester, stopping at Good Harbor Beach, where they rested to enjoy the scenery and sunset. Good Harbor is one of the Northeast's best beaches. It's long and sandy with near perfect waves rolling in from its direct exposure to the open sea. It's a neighborhood beach with year-round homes across the street. Surfers were enjoying their exclusivity that afternoon.

Blue jeans, spring jackets, and baseball caps provided all the protection from the weather they needed. They walked their bikes across the wooden bridge that divided the beach from the road and walked a little further to the small sand dunes where they sat and enjoyed the view. It was another chance to let the evaluations continue.

"It's absolutely beautiful here. How did you ever find it, and for that matter, all of the other beautiful places we have seen along the way?" asked a beaming Lexi.

"I spent a lot of time along the coast on vacation as a kid and teenager. I'm just taking you to the nicer places I remember."

"That's nice," said a pleased Lexi, who paused to drink from her bottle of water. She drew her knees up tight and rested her head on her folded arms before changing her tone to a mildly inquisitive and serious one. "This isn't by chance. You're a kind and thoughtful person. Why are you showing this to me? Only me? How is it you've remained single for so long? Were you ever married? Do you have kids? I'm asking because I'm interested, you know?"

"Let's just say I've had a few relationships over the years, one or two serious, but for various reasons, things didn't work out. I can't say more... at this time. I'm showing this to you, and only you, because I'm well, interested in you too. But let's turn the tables. Why is a beautiful woman like you single? Guys must be hitting on you all the time. You could get married every six months if you entertained proposals. Have you ever been married, got any kids?" Joe paused and stared into her soul. "Why are you here, with me?"

"I've never been married, no kids," said a serious Lexi. She looked out to where the sky and the blue sea met before eventually looking back at Joe, halfway through her reply. "Yes, where I'm from, by the time you're sixteen years old, you could be some rich guy's mistress until you got old, like twenty-one, and then move on to someone else. It all depended on how much self-respect you had. I came to Boston to go to school. Here in Boston, there are all kinds of self-declared intellectuals from the universities or finance groups offering their services and, yes, I've had quite a few of them single and married "hit on me" as you say, but I'm holding off until I meet the right guy who is broad and deep and, so far, we haven't met. Maybe."

A long kiss in the dunes overlooking the evening beach ended with a further ride to Rockport for dinner at a restaurant on picturesque Bearskin Neck. From there, it was a five-minute ride to the train station and the last train back to Boston, then a further ten-minute bicycle ride back home.

Joe did learn a little bit more about Lexi as a result of their conversation. Her professional interest in Joe was being challenged by her growing personal desire. She learned nothing new about him, already having been briefed on his personal tragedy in the Sudan.

SPRINGTIME RIDE

Spring finally made it to Boston, sometime in early May! It was common for the far suburbs to have snow into mid-April, and it wasn't too long ago that a rare early May snowstorm happened! But now, things were glorious, and Joe took every available chance to ride his bike to work instead of driving.

While biking was enjoyable, it also had its safety challenges. New England roads reflect wherever the cows wandered. They are rarely straight for more than a few hundred feet, are often cloistered in trees, and are used by motorists and pedestrians alike who up until recently, ignored the few bicyclists who dared to use them. Accidents and, unfortunately, fatalities were all too frequent.

While the ride was only four and one-half miles and twenty minutes on a good day, not even enough time to work up a good sweat or thirst, there were opportunities at every intersection for accidents. That's exactly what happened to Joe one early evening on his way home. Approaching the intersection at Hancock and Pleasant and noticing he had the protection of a green light, Joe continued forward at his measured city speed. Unseen to him was a middle-aged woman walking, but not stopping, at the corner. The woman stepped right out in front of him, engaging him, with both falling to the street. Fortunately, Joe's speed was slow, and his fall was just a few feet away.

He scraped a knee and elbow but quickly rose and went to the woman's assistance. She was a Jamaican or a Brazilian woman, one of the many that had settled in this part of Cambridge. She appeared to be in her fifties and, judging by the bags she carried, coming from recently shopping. She, too, didn't appear to be seriously injured. Joe reached out to pull her to an upright position. He asked how she was, and she answered, "Why didn't you watch where you were going?" She was wiping her brow with her headscarf when Joe replied that he was sorry he didn't see her, but he did have a green light... At this point, she cut him off. With her kerchief over her mouth, she mumbled loud enough for him to clearly hear, "Your girlfriend is a spy." She then picked up her bags and large purse and walked away.

Joe was stunned, and the meaning of what had just occurred took a while to sink in. To be clear, a woman came out of nowhere to accidentally or deliberately get into a minor accident with him and then after an expected first sentence, changed the whole dynamic of the conversation. It's possible he misheard the woman, or maybe she was a nut, or both. In any case, Joe brushed himself off, remounted his bike, and continued the ride home with a strange story to tell later after giving it all a little more thought.

TRANSITIONS

It was a Tuesday night, and Joe and Lexi were having dinner at her place followed by dessert in bed. After some relaxing sex, their thoughts returned to Cambridge. Lexi propped her elbow on the mattress and her head in her hand and asked Joe if he had found out anything new on Mansa Musa's gold. It had been awhile since she had last asked the question. She wasn't expecting his answer.

Joe said matter-of-factly," I think I know where it is, or at least some of it, and how it's being hidden. If I share my thoughts with others, however, you can bet that scavengers, government forces, and lawyers will be on it the next day, and it will do no good for mankind."

She asked him quite surprisingly, "Well, what are you going to do?"

"I've decided to go public in a big way to maximize attention to the cause. I'm participating in the International Women's Rights conference at Faneuil Hall this Friday. I'm going to speak about the abuses I saw firsthand and what needs to be done to stop them. Money is part of the solution, and I'm going to talk about funding coming from other than petro-dollars. I'm going to announce that I think I know where some of the missing gold of Mansa Musa is, and until I get ironclad agreement from the countries involved to give at least two thirds of whatever we find to women's charitable foundations in the region, I'll keep the secret to myself," replied a stone-faced Joe.

Lexi was caught off guard by this, and it showed in the surprised expression on her face. She responded in a hyper fashion, "What cause? If you know where it is, why give it all away? Keep a few billion for yourself, ourselves, and some for Harold. Who are you to give a half trillion dollars to women's studies or issues or whatever? Get real."

Joe looked at her with eyes wide open, wider than she had ever seen before and said, "It isn't for women's studies. It's for the dignity of womanhood." Lexi may have seen a fact sheet on Joe provided by her Russian leaders but didn't know the details of his engagement to a Sudanese woman. His fiancé was stoned to death for wanting to marry outside of her tribe. Killed while carrying his child and betrayed by her family doctor. This was a burden Joe continued to carry all these years later. With God as his witness, he had made a commitment to whatever he could to improve the health, education, and welfare of the region's women, all in her and his child's memory.

Shortly thereafter, Joe got dressed and went home for the night. Her reaction to his statement didn't go unnoticed by Joe. For the first time in their relationship, Lexi had blown her cool. She was no longer relaxed and at ease with the world. Suddenly, money had become important to her and Harold for some reason. *Why would her initial reaction to this also include a cut for her boss?*

Joe's announcement wasn't information Lexi could sit on. She asked for a meeting with Harold in his office the following day to discuss Joe and got right to the point.

"What's new with your boyfriend?"

"Your suspicions were correct," replied a troubled Lexi.

"He knows more about Musa than he's showing. He told me last night that he's going to speak at a woman's seminar on Friday and announce that he thinks he knows where at least some of the gold is hidden, but he isn't going to tell anyone until he gets agreement from the United Nations, the Arab League, and others that at least two thirds of the money will go to a fund to free the abused and mistreated women of the region. He isn't going to take a penny of it. I've seen the program of events, and he's on it. There was an article in yesterday's *Boston Globe* on the conference with a statement made by Joe about using the region's non-petroleum resources like gold to fund some of the actions. He's going to make an attention-grabbing public announcement to that effect."

"No one's that honest or naive. The various cultures in that part of the world won't free their women, nor will they spend their money doing it. Also, he says he's going to waive all the money? Bullshit," said an angry Harold, shaking his head in disgust.

"I begged him to keep a little for himself, for me, and for you. After all, we helped him find it," complained Lexi.

"Where is it?"

"He won't say."

"You sleep with him, and he won't tell you? He wasn't even going to tell you about the seminar in advance, was he? Good thing you asked, huh? What does that say about your future?" replied a sarcastic Harold.

Lexi, a little upset with that remark, said, "I'm secure about my future. He loves me, I'm sure."

Harold's patience was wearing thin, and he boldly and

bluntly responded, "Look, we have been generously supported by our 'friends' who, like you and me, have a real vested interest in getting our hands on at least some of this gold. They won't be happy to find out that an associate of ours, hey, your lover for Christ's sake, is going to give it all away. First, they won't believe it and second, they will cut off our stipends, and third, if they are really pissed, blow off our heads and his as well." Now he started to raise his voice.

"Who do you think sent these little rat people? Do you think it's a coincidence that they just show up here in Cambridge? You've seen what, two of them? There may be more. There could be others who look perfectly normal. Who knows? Things are getting out of control. I know you've grown attached to Joe, but for our own survival, he has to be stopped."

Lexi, now even more upset, said, "It's more than 'attached.' My feelings for him are real. I love him and have told him so, and he loves me."

"Sure, sure, like all of the others. Where and when is he planning on making his announcement, and what is he planning to say?"

"He's speaking at a seminar on women's rights at Faneuil Hall this Friday afternoon. I think he is just going to make a general announcement with no specifics, but you never know what he'll do."

"Faneuil Hall? What a showoff. This guy is half-cooked." Harold got quiet for a few seconds, and the tone of his voice morphed to that of an inert, cold-hearted assassin. He coolly and calmly said, "That's right, you never know.

Some truth serum could loosen him up in the weeks and months ahead. So, you have a choice; get some truth serum into him in the next few days ahead of who knows who else, so we have the answers, and then kill him, or just kill him. It's your decision but do it quickly and act accordingly. You're a trained agent and know what has to be done." It was as if he was talking to a child.

She walked out of Harold's office stunned and shaken. She had never heard him talk like that. She was an experienced agent and knew what had to be done and how to do it. Late that evening, she called Joe very upset. She had just heard from a colleague that Harold had died a few hours earlier in his apartment of an apparent drug overdose.

THURSDAY NIGHT

Joe was at Lexi's apartment. They had just returned from a quick and quiet dinner near her office. They were both upset over Harold's death. While Lexi fiddled around her kitchen, Joe sat on the sofa, quietly staring at the corners of her living room, nursing a drink in his hand. His staring grew more intense and measured. "I know I've said it before, honey, but this is a gorgeous apartment. Nice location, nice furniture, great kitchen. How can you afford it?"

"Just lucky, I guess. It's rent-controlled."

"Wow. And how did you get a permanent work visa so fast?"

"I don't know, lucky I guess there too. Harvard is an

important place, you know. Why are you suddenly asking so many questions?"

"Oh, I don't know. It's just that I've been sitting here and thinking, and there are things I can't figure out. You live in an apartment I can't afford, and I'm making a lot of money. By the way, rent control was abolished many years ago, so someone wanted you to have this apartment, and that was a convenient excuse. You've told me about your family, and they seem to be real nice people, but you have no photos of them. I've been in every room of your apartment and have seen nothing. Do you have any photos you could show me? You have a work permit that's difficult to get, even with serious sponsorship, but you weren't working at Harvard then. You were working at some small outfit in Boston.

"You recalled every detail of the trivia night at Murphy's for no apparent reason. Some black woman walks into my bike two weeks ago and tells me that my girlfriend is a spy. Weird, huh? You knew about the tiger children but never told me. Oh, and Harold, I found him to be an interesting and helpful guy. I was shocked when you called me last night to tell me he overdosed. Did you know he was a drug addict?"

"No, I didn't. I was shocked," replied a serious Lexi, who was now tensed up and sitting beside Joe.

"Not as shocked as I was. You called me at midnight, but the police put the time of death at two a.m. His heart kept beating, ever so slowly, for at least another two hours. I guess the drugs were slow acting, huh?" After a long pause, Joe leaned over and looked her straight in the eyes and asked, "Who are you, and you had better be honest and tell me fast. I've got too much invested in this relationship to be lied to."

With tearing eyes, Lexi said, "I'm a confused girl who is in love with you with all of my heart and will do anything to protect you. You need to believe me. Harold and I officially held Harvard positions that are known, but we also 'consulted' for various entities. I don't know who they are by name. All I do know is that I receive a separate consulting check every month from this company and a commission from Harold. There could be others doing this as well; I don't know.

"You're right, my Harvard salary wouldn't cover half of this apartment, but my stipend from the others more than made up the difference. These people also pay for my brother's health care costs back in the Ukraine at a private and expensive facility. Without their help, he would be a near vegetable in a government-run facility for poor farmers. Death would be a better option at that point."

"What do they want from you?"

"Data, information, and any stolen treasures we come across. There's big money in stolen antiquities. They have also had this long-time fantasy about Mansa Musa's gold. Joe, one-half trillion dollars disappeared. Do you know how many uprisings, politicians, castles, and causes, or old-world masters' paintings that kind of money can buy?

"Give me, give us, a fraction of a percent of this gold, and we could live like royalty forever. I told Harold of your plan to give the money to the women of the world. He said our sponsors would feel that he and I had double-crossed them and kill us both, and you. He said that they had most likely sent these rat people or whoever they are to stop you, and he told me that I knew what must be done. Ironically, he was right."

It took Joe a few seconds to grasp what he had just been told. "You killed Harold?" asked a shocked Joe.

"People that work for me did it. They're professionals; it was clean." Incredibly, she said this calmly, with any emotion drained from her face.

"People that work for you? Jesus Christ, now I'm really confused. Are these people that 'work for you' different from the people that you and he consult for? Can I assume they aren't Harvard employees?" said a now angry, excited, and sarcastic Joe.

"It's complicated. Harold told me to kill you. I love you. If I didn't love you, I would have killed you. Please believe me. You're in danger. Please don't go to Faneuil Hall on Friday. I don't know who will be there or what they will do. Call it all off. Say it was a mistake. Please." Tears now dripped from Lexi's face.

There was a monstrous struggle going in Joe's head between the emotions of reason and trust. Reason forced the issue and made Joe ask one more fateful question, "Who is Michael?"

The effect on Lexi was the same as a bucket of cold water to her face. She froze for a few seconds, and those few seconds sealed her fate.

"He's just a friend, an old friend. How do you know him?"

"Oh, only by text messages that occasionally pop up on

your cell phone. Oh look, here's a new one that popped up while you were in the bathroom. I'd say he's more than a close friend. Here." He passed the phone to her to read.

Lexi didn't know what to say, but Joe did. He shook his head and said, "I have to go," and got up from the sofa and walked out of her apartment into the night.

Lexi sat there alone for what appeared to be the longest time, trying to rationally sort through in her mind what she should do next. She too was struggling, with reality versus fantasy, love versus lust, comfort versus anxiety, her family versus loneliness. She had deeply hurt the one person who honestly cared for her, and he had just walked out the door.

FANEUIL HALL

Faneuil Hall is of great importance in American history, often referred to as the "cradle of liberty." This large brick building was built in 1742 by prominent Boston business-man, Peter Faneuil, and donated to the city of Boston as a place where merchants could sell their wares in one common area. Famous early revolutionary speeches and meetings were held in its large, great hall.

From this meeting room, the "Indians" marched to the nearby harbor to destroy tea that had just arrived by ship as a protest of the outrageous stamp act taxes that the king of England had placed on most imports to pay for his recent war with France. The "Boston Tea Party" went down in American history as one of the first acts of defiance against the oppressive British rule.

Over the years, many other famous meetings had been held in this imposing hall. The seminar had received a lot of attention through social media and the many university organizations in the city. As a matter of routine, the networks sent their local affiliates, the social media their local stringers, and other interested parties were also in attendance. Security was the standard for a small event, which were two policemen. The hall is on the second floor of the building with the first floor still used by various merchants. Behind the stage of the hall is a huge oil portrait of Daniel Webster replying to Senator Hayne. Flanking the portrait are two smaller oil portraits, one of George Washington and the other of Peter Faneuil. As in many old New England churches and meeting halls, there are balconies on either side of the hall and at the rear as well.

Joe had let his teammates and boss know broadly what he was doing that afternoon and why, but not the specifics. Several decided to also leave work at noon to find out what was going on. Lexi was also in the crowd, nervously walking and looking around, not knowing who or what she was looking for. Keeping a low profile in the wings on either side of the hall were two tiger children. Several dozen tourists wandered in, along with one hundred members of various local women's groups. Lexi saw Joe at the side of the stage and made one more attempt to convince him to cancel his announcement. "Leave me alone," was his simple and unemotional reply.

The program began precisely at two p.m. Joe was the sixth speaker on the program. When it was his turn, he walked to the podium and looked over the crowd. This was it. He began the meeting by introducing himself and thanking everyone for attending, and then quickly progressed into the heart of his presentation, an eye-witness account of various cruelties, and what must be done to stop them, and correct the damages they had caused.

"What is required here is more than a change of cultures. Vast amounts of money are needed to fund health care, education, food and water, housing, and other glaring needs. Petro-dollars can fund some of this but many of these countries have no oil or gas resources. It's ironic, however, that some of the most deprived countries in this region have some of the greatest wealth, which up until now has been hidden. Gold! You probably think the richest man who ever lived on this earth is some currently living high-tech person whose name you've seen in the news or his face on television.

"A second guess may be John D. Rockefeller. This isn't the case. The truth is that a man, who lived and died almost seven hundred years ago in Africa, holds that title. His name was Mansa Musa, and he had at one time a fortune esti-mated to be worth more than five hundred billion dollars. No one knew where much of it went, until now. As a result of recent research, I now feel with a great deal of certainty that a significant amount of this fortune has been in the North African region, but its specific locations not yet revealed.

"The fortune could be ready to be put to good use, but I'm insisting on a singular purpose, to free the women of the world. For far too many centuries, women have been treated in some parts of the world as property, to be used and abused as their male or female owner saw fit. This form of slavery must stop, and now. As with sunken treasure, you just can't go and take it without resolving its legal ownership.

"I'll soon begin discussions with the various countries in Africa and the Mid-East, which is where this bounty resides, to resolve the ownership issue. This will be done in cooperation with the United Nations. I won't reveal the locations, or any details required to access the fortune until agreement is reached on the portion to be claimed by the local country with the balance to be given to a United Nations fund devoted entirely to the welfare of the women of this part of the world. I've already been told unofficially that this will be impossible due to various reasons, but those are my terms. I can tell you with certainty that..."

The tiger boys had heard enough. As soon as they heard the word "gold," they were on high alert. Fearing he would say too much more, the first ran out from the sideline and fired several shots that hit Joe in the chest. Joe turned to stare at him and then after a few burning seconds, dropped to the floor unconscious at the podium. Screams and shouts erupted from the people in the audience.

Lexi's formal "training" was now put to use. She broke from the sideline as well and from a distance, she fired a semi-automatic pistol multiple times, killing the first shooter. The second gunman was on the opposite side of the hall. He also ran out and shot at Joe, hitting him in the legs as he fell to the ground. He then turned and fired multiple shots toward Lexi, one or more hitting her in the head, killing her instantly. Several seminar attendees were injured in the melee as well.

Sanjib saw all of this going on and ran from his position down in front of the hall and tackled the second shooter who wrestled himself free from Sanjib's grip. He saw the police coming at him, yelling for him to drop the gun, but he felt he had to finish off Sanjib first. He shot twice and seriously wounded Sanjib, as he tried to scramble away. Before he could shoot again, he was shot and seriously wounded by a policeman.

Ambulances took them all away to nearby Massachusetts General Hospital (MGH). That evening, all the forms of mass communication were devoted to this bizarre turn of events. The news had now generated much more interest and credibility for the topic.

EIGHT

The Recovery

Joe and Sanjib spent a lot of time in recovery in a privately guarded rehabilitation facility located away from Cambridge. It was favored by celebrities who didn't want prying press to see them in unflattering conditions. In a previous life, it was the weekend Georgian style mansion of a Boston industrialist. Now, it was an oasis of privacy and seclusion for its twenty-five guests. They were under police protection, given the odd circumstances of the shootings and the fact they were working on a secret military project.

Both were fortunate that while their wounds were serious, nothing vital was hit or severely damaged. Sanjib's family visited frequently, which boosted his spirits. Nara came to visit both of them on a regular basis, too. In time, they could play with the kids on the estate's large lawns, completely unnoticed by the passing cars and trucks hundreds of yards away down the estate's driveway and on the other side of a large and imposing iron fence.

Joe's position was different. He had no family. Lexi and

the tiger children were now dead. One was still alive when brought to MGH, where he lingered for a few days before dying. The doctors couldn't determine a blood type for him or his dead partner. There were too many minerals and isotopes in his blood to make a determination. The FBI was now involved and arguing with the MGH staff over this issue. A recent meeting at the hospital between them was heated.

The head FBI agent barked at the lead doctor, "We need to know who this guy is and where he is from ASAP. What's wrong with your tests?"

The lead doctor responded with equal anger in his voice, "You bring in here some little creep from Munimula, no blood type, and screwed-up eyes, and you're asking me what's wrong? Did he or the dead one have a passport or driver's license?"

"It appears their documentation was forged. On the surface, everything was in order but when we tried to verify any of it, there was nothing to back it up. They were using the data of dead people. We have asked for a court order to conduct an autopsy on the dead one and, if this guy dies, an autopsy on him as well," replied a now more contrite FBI agent.

The media was now poking around a lot. Why would a nobody like Joe make what could very well be a crackpot speech at Faneuil Hall about women's rights and hidden gold and then suffer an attempted assassination, during which several others were seriously wounded and two more die.

Taking it further, why did a woman research assistant

from Harvard kill one of the odd-looking characters and then get shot and killed by the other one, and her boss overdosed or murdered (depending on who you believe) just days earlier? The tabloids went wild with hypotheses of who was involved and where the gold was hidden. China, high-tech companies, the Russians, everyone was suspect.

Work on the Pokey project was continued but at a much slower pace with two of their key people in recovery. Secrecy was a bigger issue with more than the usual parties being suspected. Now there were activists of all kinds and various religious groups also interested as an influx of a possible several hundred billion dollars could have a huge effect on the furthering of various programs, not to mention terrorist activities around the world.

NSA INTERVIEW

Meeting inside Joe's recovery room one week after the shooting were two NSA people, two FBI agents, and Joe's boss, Skip. The FBI people looked like your stereotypical baggy-pants agents, while the NSA reps could have passed as investment bankers. The lead NSA agent was forty years old, five feet ten inches in height, trim, well-groomed, and well dressed. His sharp nose and closely set eyes were complemented by thin gold glasses and a full head of dark hair with a sharp part on the left. At various times in his career, Joe had to deal with these people, and it was rarely pleasant. As if their cold smiles weren't enough, their personalities displayed another side of them... sarcastic, curt, and condescending.

The lead NSA agent began the barrage, "Okay, Joe, please explain to us how a secret assignment could go so far astray. You were hired to help explore faster ways to detect movement primarily in difficult terrain, yet you somehow twisted this into a search to find King Midas' gold and in the process, get three to five people killed, create some wild stories for the tabloids with your women's program, and, more importantly, possibly exposing our entire much larger top-secret program to the world! What the hell were you thinking about?"

Joe ignored the harassment and calmly asked, "How's Sanjib?"

The second NSA agent (in a firm tone) said, "He's recovering in the next room. Your lover, the Russian spy, is dead; the two guys from somewhere in Africa are dead; and, of course, you already knew that her boss died a mysterious, questionable death." He calmed down, and his tone became pleasant and soothing. "Other than that, the world is fine." His sarcasm continued. Raising his eyebrows, he asked, "How about them Red Sox?"

Joe still couldn't accept or believe this. "What do you mean she was a spy?" he asked in a weak voice. He closed his eyes for a second and shook his head. He was obviously a little groggy from some medication.

The lead NSA agent jumped in again, "Come on, with all of your training and contacts, you didn't know she was a spy? You couldn't see it? Your dick must have been in the way. Shit, we had one of our agents try to warn you. Do you remember hitting the black chick with your bike near Memorial Drive?"

The other NSA agent switched to playing the "good cop" and, in a calm and even tone, said, "She was actually a good spy. She shot and killed the guy that shot you first. She saved your life. We have checked her out. She came here ten years ago officially on a student visa, granted because of phony credentials and a phony personal history suitable for the soap operas. Someone fixed it so she could stay permanently with forged documents.

"We're checking into that. Her boss was a double spy, working for the Russians as well, and for another unidentified foreign interest group involved in smuggling African antiquities. She would assist him in that on occasion. We don't know who they are, but we're investigating that, too. He didn't know it, but she was his superior within the Russian spy chain. Part of her job was to keep an eye on him."

One of the FBI agents watching all of this decided to chime right in sarcastically, "Boy, you guys are right on top of everything!" He gave a thumb's up sign.

The lead NSA agent looked at him and shot back, "Put a cork in it, flatfoot. This all happened domestically, three miles from your office. Don't you have some traffic tickets to fix, or bookies to shake down?"

Joe shook his head and spoke slowly, "It's all a coincidence. I was researching materials for our study when things just fell into place. The richest guy in the world came from a trivia question at a bar. He was African and had travelled in many of the same areas we're looking at." After a pause, he continued, muttering under his breath, "And God, she was beautiful."

"Where is the gold, Joe?" bluntly asked the lead NSA agent.

"Beats the shit out of me," shot back an angry Joe, losing his cool.

"What?"

"Beats the shit out of me, sir!" Joe's slow burn had flashed into a rage. "I don't know for sure, but I have a pretty good hunch, and I'm not telling anyone until I get an iron-clad agreement from all of the parties involved that, yes, the bulk of it will go to saving/freeing/helping the women of that part of the world. If that's not going to happen, the money will stay right where it is for another thousand years." Tempers were flaring all around.

"Who appointed you God when it comes to saving the women of the world?" shouted the second NSA agent.

Joe nearly screamed, exasperated and almost out of control, "I did! I saw it first-hand. I've seen the suffering, the beatings, the mutilation, and the killings. I suffered from it firsthand. It has to stop!" He began to cry and covered his eyes with his left hand. His outburst caused him both mental and physical pain.

The lead NSA agent took control of the situation and in a calmer voice, said, "Okay, everyone, let's calm down. Can you think of anything you would have told Lexi or Harold that may in any way big or small, compromise the Pokey project or any people?

His response was a curt, "No."

After a short pause, the lead NSA agent said, "Okay,

that's enough for today. You've drawn too much attention to our program already. We don't want your moves and our every move followed and analyzed. As of now, you and Sanjib are off the program and have been reassigned to another program outside of the Boston area that removes you entirely from what's going on. Your personal belongings are being moved from the office to your homes today. The program will continue but probably at a slower pace for a while."

The second FBI agent said, "It's likely that numerous people will try to reach you either for an interview, or to make a deal for a piece of the golden pie. We're going to keep our eyes on you for a while. Here is our number in case you want to contact us. Chances are we won't be too far away." He reached out to Joe and gave him a business card.

The lead NSA agent said, "You need to know what you've gotten into. You got someone's major attention with this poking around. Someone sent those guys to watch and/or stop you. We have had an extensive autopsy conducted on both of their bodies. They were a bit unique."

It was all going in but not registering. Joe rested his head on his pillow and gazed at the ceiling. For the first time in years, he had started to feel safe, secure, and loved again. Now, all of it was all gone in a flash.

Nara's Visit

Joe and Sanjib's recoveries took a long time. Although they were receiving the best of care, they were, as might be expected, frustrated and eager to go home. Nara came to visit each of them again during the second week, this time with questions for Joe.

"Hi, how are you feeling today?" she asked with a restrained smile.

"Hi, Nara, each day a little bit better. Thanks for stopping by. I'm getting fidgety, however, and want out of here as soon as possible. I need a beer! I imagine Sanjib is the same."

"Of course. He misses his family. I brought you something." It was a cup of Dunkin Donuts coffee and two donuts, a New England staple. Joe pounced on them. "Has anyone from your family been in to see you?"

"No, they haven't. I really have none. I was a late-in-life surprise, and both of my parents have passed away. I have a much older sister living in upstate New York, but she suffers from early onset Alzheimer's and barely knows who I am. She can't come."

"I see. Joe, there's something serious I need to discuss with you. While you and Sanjib have been here, funeral services were held for Harold in the campus chapel. They were conducted by his church minister, and he was buried in his hometown. We didn't know anything about Lexi, so we had the hospital's chaplain perform a basic service for her before her body was moved to the city morgue. I'm sorry you couldn't attend."

"Thank you for doing that. I would have liked to but…" He lifted both hands from his side and dropped them in an expression of frustration. His eyes welled up.

"We don't know anything about her. She has no family of record here or back in the Ukraine. We don't know what to do with her body, so it's still in the city morgue. I thought it best to get your opinion before suggesting anything to the city. Did she ever mention family or final arrangements? I know this is awkward, but we don't know what else to do. Her only relationships were with the school and you."

"She did speak of her family back in the city of Kiev, but no mention of dying. Shit, she hadn't even begun to live."

"Yes, we checked out the family names she put in her personnel file at work but none of them exist, at least now. It appears she was completely alone in this world, except for you. This is a difficult question to ask you, but what do you think we should do with her remains?"

"You're hitting me up with a lot to think about in a hurry. Can you give me a day to think about it? I'll give you a call."

"Sure."

He looked at Nara and saw a woman of great internal strength. She had lost her husband not too much earlier, and now she was visiting her brother-in-law who almost passed away as well.

Joe asked, "How are you doing?"

"Hanging in there," she said, with her lips pursed and

clenched shut and slightly nodding her head. "Eventually, things will calm down, and life will return to some semblance of normalcy. I'm sure of it." He could see a tear in her eye and her head continuing with the slight reassuring nod.

"There were a lot of things you didn't know about her or Harold. She was a nice girl with a cloudy past. I'm in Human Resources, and I've seen her personnel file. There were a lot of blanks and misinformation in it. She must have had powerful connections to get a permanent visa as quickly as she did. I've seen Harold's file too. Everyone knew he was from old North Shore Yankee money. He squandered his share of the family fortune on wine, women, men, and drugs. He had a serious drug habit that cost him several wives and lots of money to service, and even more money to keep quiet. It also appears that he was involved in selling stolen antiquities on a large scale. I don't understand how that was kept quiet for so long. You would expect the local museums and universities would have been made aware of that long ago."

"You know, I was always careful with what I told Lexi or anyone for that matter. General things like I'm working on a government study, farm aid stuff, and I was chosen because of my experience in that area, etc. No details were ever passed to anyone."

"Okay, that's good," said Nara. "Well, I've got to go. I'll see you later, and don't forget to call and give me your instructions for Lexi."

Joe thanked her very much for visiting him and told her how much it meant to him. He also made a mental note to somehow thank her appropriately after he had been released.

He spent the balance of the day thinking about his time with Lexi. Why did he ignore the warning signs that were there from the beginning? It was obvious she and Michael were at least part-time lovers but he really felt she loved him, at least a little. He had to ignore the angst that came with knowing that if he had acted on his earlier suspicions, she would still be alive today.

He also had to think where she might want her final resting place to be. The following day, he called Nara and suggested that Lexi's body be cremated, and her ashes given to him. He then arranged for her ashes to be spread from an airplane flying low over Mount Washington, where he and she could return in the years to come to check out the status of those coins they had found in the rocks one frosty August morning.

Nara's Home

Nara returned to her small five-room home in nearby Arlington. It was a simple home with three rooms on the first floor and two bedrooms upstairs. A narrow garage at the end of a cement driveway built to house a Ford Model T car sat in the back of the lot. It was barely large enough to house her Honda Accord. She hung up her jacket and prepared a quiet dinner for one. The television news provided some background noise for what otherwise would be a somber period of her day.

Life had been quiet since her husband Ravi's death some months earlier. Without family of her own in America, her solace was her brother-in-law's wife and children. As much as she adored children, Nara had none of her own. This wasn't due to any physical limitation, but to a strong feeling of only bringing up children in a home with a committed husband and wife unit.

Her intelligence provided her the exit from the Sudan. While she loved her parents and extended family very much and would return home every two years for a visit, the chances of a good life in the Sudan were dim with continuing civil strife. Attending university in the United States and graduating cum laude opened doors for her to stay. It led to a senior position in the Human Resources Department at Harvard University.

She met Ravi Patel at a social gathering arranged by the local chapter of the Indian Society. Greater Boston has over the years, attracted many Indian nationals to the region's financial, high-tech, and educational facilities. With over seventy-five thousand Indian nationals living in the region, the opportunity to meet and mate with one of your religious or social equals were high. As a new arrival in the United States, Nara wanted to preserve as much of her "Indian side" as possible as she transitioned from one culture to another. It's questionable if it worked.

Nara was a reserved, strong-willed woman. In her marriage to Ravi, however, she settled. Half the dream was better than none of the dream, and that's what marriage to Ravi was all about. It was a loveless relationship. Nara was approaching her mid-thirties when they married, a point in

Indian culture where a woman's prospects for marriage were slim. Nara feared being alone, like now.

Ravi was certainly respected as an engineering manager and back in India, he did come from a respected, though not necessarily high caste, but he was boring, quiet, and withdrawn. He was polite and kind to Nara to be sure, but he wasn't social and had no interest in having children. His life would be his work... a lifestyle, or more appropriately, "fate" Nara would have to accept and share, in silence.

Dinner tonight in their small kitchen would be typical Indian dishes that Nara would make in quantity on a Sunday and consume over the course of the week. Favorites like chicken korma, dal, and pilaf were tasty night after night and, of course, accompanied by raita, a soothing yogurt and cucumber dish. She was well-taught by her mother how to prepare healthy and flavorful Indian and Sudanese dishes with just the right balance of spices. On occasion, like tonight, however, the addition of a few tears made the meal a little bitter.

NINE

Autopsy

Joe had a compelling reason to see the full autopsies of the two gunmen killed at Faneuil Hall. Shortly after getting out of the rehab center, he telephoned Frank O'Malley, the FBI regional head, upon his return to Boston.

"Hello Frank. How are you doing?"

"Good morning, Joe. I'm fine, thank you. How are you feeling? What can I do for you?"

"I'm feeling a lot better, thanks. I need a favor. I'm trying to figure who the strange murderers were, and I need a lot more details about them. I would like to see their full autopsy reports. I feel they could help explain a lot."

"No can do, Joe. That's privileged information that can only be released to their families. Sorry."

"That's great news. When did their families come forward?"

This caused Frank to stammer a bit, "Well, actually no one came forward, so the local Orthodox Church agreed to bury them."

"I see. So, they were Christian; how about that. Well, then can I come into your office and view the report? I can take notes of anything I consider important."

"Still can't help you as the information is part of an ongoing investigation and is also classified."

Joe was now getting a little annoyed at Frank's stalling tactics. "Frank, I know all about the ongoing investigation; it's about the attempted murder of me for Christ's sake. You know I have the security clearances. You can either let me see the documents, or I'll call Washington to instruct you to release them. I don't want to make a big deal about this."

Frank paused a few seconds and then said, "Okay, when do you want to come in?"

"Tomorrow morning at nine."

"See you then."

Joe arrived at the O'Neill Federal Building promptly at nine a.m. the next day with a notepad in hand. Once in Frank's office on the twelfth floor, he sat down and read. The first autopsy was revealing.

Age: Estimated 20-25 years old

Height: Five foot five inches

Weight: One hundred thirty-five pounds

Blood Type: Unknown (See note one)

Race: Caucasian

Skin tone: Light brown

Hair color: Brown

Eye color: Brown (See note two)

Unique physical features:

- Subject has a slightly elongated head and ears.

- Subject has an enlarged chest cavity and lungs, which would make him potentially adaptable to living at higher elevations than a normal person could handle. The lung capacity was roughly like the indigenous people of the Andes Mountains/Kenya/Tibet/Ethiopia.

Note #1- Subject's blood color was normal but didn't register as any of the previously recognizable types (O, A, B, AB or positive / negative). The blood analysis contained many chemical traces (some toxic, some radioactive) that could have a serious debilitating effect on lifespan.

Note #2- While examining the subject's eyes, it was noted that each lacked an iris, a condition called aphakia. In cases like this, the subject is often not able to focus as well as non-sufferers and can also see below the normal human color spectrum and into the ultraviolet range of colors.

Personal Belongings

1. Fake driver's license (Massachusetts)
2. Fake green card
3. Fake social security number
4. Five hundred dollars in cash
5. A credit card

The file on the other gunman was similar other than the driver's license (New Jersey) and the amount of cash ($235). He did have one piece of personal property that the other did not, a cross with a small inscription on it. The inscription had been translated from the original Aramaic to English – Jesus Christ, Lord and Savior."

Joe asked Frank, "What is the closest thing you've worked on in the past to this one? These people are from another planet."

"I've seen plenty of gangland killings but nothing like this."

"Have you ever seen blood types like this?"

"No. I've seen cases of blood poisoning where it took months to pull it off. Nothing as dramatic as these two guys!"

"Has there been any interest in picking up the bodies?"

"None. No family, no friends. As I said, the Orthodox Church took care of things for us and buried them in their cemetery. What they had listed as their place of work is fraudulent as well."

"How about their landlords?"

"It's hard to track down a fictitious owner on a fictitious street at a fictitious address!"

"Gotcha. Thanks, Frank. I'll let you know if I find anything interesting." Joe left and went back to Cambridge.

More things were coming together. The storyteller spoke of their cat-like eyes and special diet and waters. Now Joe learned they suffered from aphakia, a condition where a person has no iris in their eyes. This condition can exist due to genetic issues, damage to the eyes, or an operation. The iris has several functions. One is to improve the focusing of the eye. People with aphakia are usually farsighted, i.e., they can't see objects up close as would be expected with normal vision. They usually also have small pupils. The other is to filter out infrared light which, if it enters the internal of the eye directly, it could burn it.

Without the iris, it has been reported that people can see some portions of the infrared spectrum of light. Pablo Picasso is a famous example. After he had cataract surgery on his eyes at age eighty-three, he reportedly could see into the infrared spectrum and began painting different shades of white and purple. People with aphakia have been used to read secret messages transmitted in UV light. During World War II, the U.S. government positioned people with aphakia at several locations along the U.S. East Coast to intercept any messages being sent by German U-boats via UV light to agents onshore.

The special foods and waters could have helped maintain this genetic deficiency or create it or had some other benefits. There are chemicals and enzymes found in various forms of wildlife (birds are an example) that help these creatures see in the ultraviolet range. They also help these same creatures to give off ultraviolet light. In any case, it may be these "supplements" are responsible for the absence of a measurable blood type. They could be highly toxic and help account for the short lifespan.

HANSCOM

Joe and Sanjib had been transferred as promised by the NSA out of the Pokey project into support positions on other defense programs. Eastern New England is the home to over one hundred universities and colleges, with over fifty with international fame. Harvard, MIT, Holy Cross, Tufts, Dartmouth, Brown, Boston College, Worcester Polytech, Boston University, Northeastern, the list goes on and on.

There are hundreds of government contractors in the region as well. The government could have found Sanjib and Joe homes at any one of them that accept government contracts.

The government did them a favor by placing them at the nearby Hanscom Air Base in Bedford, Massachusetts. Bedford is located fifteen miles northwest of Cambridge, just north of Interstate 95. The actual Air Force base was transferred years earlier to the State of Massachusetts for use as a civilian airport, but many Air Force R&D activities were still being carried out there as a result of the research firms and universities in the area. There were ten thousand civilian and military workers on base, handling a multitude of programs.

There was military security at the gates and perimeters of the base, and it was a good spot for the two to have been placed as it was a thirty-minute commute for both of them. Neither had to relocate, but both were bored silly. They had gone from being leaders in an interesting secret project for the U.S. military to passive paper pushers in the back office of late stage projects. For them, for now, it was nothing more than the same paycheck for little meaningful work.

Joe was now more alone than ever. His only daily contact had been Sanjib, with whom he spent time every day while they were hospitalized. Contact dropped off after they were released but continued on a regular basis now that they were working in Hanscom, even though they were on different programs in different buildings on the same campus. It was no longer walking into the next office or hospital room to have a cup of coffee or tea and chat about things big or small.

Sanjib did invite him to a family get together. He invited Nara as well. Whether it was due to mutual need or respect, there was a growing relationship between them. They found strength and comfort in each other during this healing process and spent time together on personal activities. It started slowly, attending civic events like charities or museum openings. In time, it grew to obvious personal events, like dinner and shows.

CLIMBING MT. AFRICA

Joe's move to the Hanscom Air Base R&D operations placed him in a company with a lucrative telecommunications contract with the U.S. Air Force.

The company's name was Sixfold Defense Industries, or "Sixfold" for short. It was a Lexington, MA military contractor founded twenty years earlier to take advantage of the continual expected improvements in advanced radar technologies. Sixfold was the prevailing thought on the magnitude of performance improvement for the future. Whether they knew it or not, Joe's placement in their offices would be quite fortuitous.

It wasn't unusual in the defense world to have an unknown body just dumped on you from out of the blue as a "consultant." Those who had been around for a while knew enough just to say okay and find the new person a respectable office and clerical support, and not expect too much from them. Many, if not most, of these newly found consultants were either a relative or a friend of a politician, someone who had just retired from the military and needed a home for a few more years until full retirement, or someone who had screwed up badly elsewhere.

For this reason, no one within Sixfold management blinked an eye when Joe showed up unannounced. There was even less of a reason when it became known that he had multiple top-secret clearances. No one knew who he might really be or with what authority.

Sixfold had recently received a substantial contract to upgrade multiple United States listening/radar posts around the world. Their locations were secret for obvious reasons, but occasionally word of their placement would leak out. Some of the sites to be upgraded were in North Africa and the Middle East.

Somehow, word leaked to Sixfold management of Joe's previous unique experience in that part of the world. Unique in this case was an understatement given that he not only worked there, lived there, spoke several of the local languages, and had installed similar equipment on several of the same mountains twelve years ago. It made Joe valuable to Sixfold. There were some in management who thought Joe had been planted in their offices by agreement between top management and the government.

Sixfold's program manager Drew Thomas and project director Nessie Khat decided to approach Joe on accepting a position with their team. A casual meeting was held in the company's main cafeteria.

"Joe, we could use your help on a unique program," said Drew. "You already know what it is we make and do. Because you maintain multiple high-level security clearances, we can go into greater detail with you. Our contract is to remove and/or upgrade twenty-three listening and radar sites around the world. The new equipment has a greater range and sensitivity, is more compact, and can be remotely disabled or even destroyed if required. Four of the sites are in the Arabic/Muslim region of the world at high altitudes.

"We recently became aware of your previous experience in the region with similar listening devices and to be quite honest with you, we're a bit blown away. I have one Arabic-speaking Egyptian on my team and two alpine skiers, but no one with your breadth of experience."

At this point, Joe cut him off. "Hold on, what do you want?" he questioned suspiciously.

"We would like you to join our team as a consultant, to assist with the project, as necessary. I won't hide anything from you. We would need you to go to the region and climb the mountains and help with the install and commissioning. Advanced teams have already located protected sites and prepared the foundations. Mounting bolts are already in place, so that part of the work is done.

"It isn't easy work, and it will require a lot of time away from home, but it comes with a hazardous duty bonus allowance, so there's a chance to make a lot of money in a non-war zone environment."

Joe's answer was quick and curt, "Thanks, but I'm not interested. Been there and done that."

Nessie jumped into the conversation, "Joe, if you took the assignment, you would be helping your country and escaping what must be a boring job. If I can be honest with you, I've seen a lot of people dumped here as a favor to someone or a place to hang out. You don't appear to be a person who's looking for a place to hide for the next twenty-five years." Joe said nothing in reply.

After an awkward silence, Drew said, "Okay, if that's your decision, I'll respect it. Given your experience, I hope you won't mind if our people come over occasionally and ask you a few questions about the region. I would appreciate it if you would think on it overnight or over the weekend and let me know if your position has changed. We could use you."

Joe nodded okay, they shook hands, and everyone went back to their desks. Back in his apartment that night, all alone with a glass of wine in hand, he thought it over. He was bored. Bored to tears. He was in a made-up job to hide him away while the whole Pokey thing blew over. He could be there for years, pushing papers.

While he still maintained some social life, he was also lonely.

If he agreed to join the team, it would be challenging (as it was twelve years earlier), financially rewarding, and would give him an opportunity to poke around a few of the mountaintops where Mansa Musa may have hidden his treasures. He might have a chance to decide once and for all if it was possible to hide the treasures, and if in fact it was done.

If the riches were hidden on any of these mountains, it might allow Joe to pursue his commitment to the local women. It might also allow him a backdoor way to rejoin the Pokey team. He called Drew the next morning.

"I've reconsidered and am interested in joining your team, provided I'm authorized to carry a sidearm at all times. It will be a sidearm of my choice, and ammunition will be provided to me by the program. I had one in previous assignments in the region and if anything has changed, it's for the worse. No gun-no deal."

"Okay, I think we can accept that. Well, this is great. I'll let Nessie know. You'll be a direct report to me and assist her and others as needed. I'll get the paperwork going. Thanks, and welcome aboard."

HIGH TRAINING

With the agreement in place, he began a two-month training program to acclimate himself to higher altitudes. The team met for the first time with only two members of Sixfold and Joe knowing one another. It was a six-man team led by an Air Force colonel with experience in similar clandestine operations in the region. His name was Scott Gordon.

Scott was an interesting fellow. He was slightly taller than Joe, and equally handsome. His hair, eyes, and round head gave every indication of Central Asian ancestry, but he hailed from Wyoming. His previous training was like Joe's. It was expected that he, too, could be thrown from the back of a truck and survive on whatever the land could provide. He also had substantial experience in the region of interest.

Other team members included an ex-Marine for extra security named Riley, a systems engineer, a software engineer, and a radar expert.

Joe had gone through similar training twelve years ago, but a refresher was in order as the capability went away over time.

The first month of training was held in Colorado at the United States Air Force Academy. While there was some classroom training in basic electronics and Arabic, a major goal was to acclimate their lungs and circulatory systems to the elevated altitude. The academy is in Boulder, Colorado, at an elevation of fifty-four hundred feet above sea level. This is the same elevation as some of the base camps they would be using in the region.

Altitude acclimation is essential training. There are four broad altitude regions recognized by medical authorities for their effect on human ability to survive. The high-altitude category covers heights from five to eleven thousand feet. The effect on humans in this range can vary all the way from high altitude sickness to death. Very high altitude covers approximately eleven to eighteen thousand feet.

At fifteen thousand feet, most people start to faint due to the lack of oxygen in the air. Experienced climbers can push higher because they gradually acclimate their bodies to the drop in oxygen.

The second month of training was specific to the project. There were discussions of what each assignment involved, how each would be executed, the terrain (and here was where Joe could directly contribute), and what the protocols were if the project had to be aborted or something else went horribly wrong. The newest generation radars were incredible.

Smaller, lightweight, and more powerful with some having more than a fifteen-hundred-mile range, they transmitted up to satellites and not down to land stations below. They could also be disabled and destroyed remotely from above as well. The four mountains in the region to be worked on were:

- Mount Stanley - Uganda - 17,000 ft.
- Ras Dashen - Ethiopia -15,000 ft.
- Emi Koussi - Chad - 11,300 ft.
- Jebel Marra - Sudan – 10,200 ft.

From these four locations, all of northeast Africa from Tunisia to Mozambique could be effectively covered for major aviation activities, including missiles. Joe quickly noticed that three of the four mountains were on the trans-Saharan travel routes used for hundreds of years to move salt, gold, and slaves from east to west.

It had been a long time, but he was excited about something again. The team had been given an extended weekend off after four weeks to return home and see their families. Joe used the time to take care of any local business he had and to see Nara, the only female he had contact with.

He was growing fond of her but not sure of her position with him. Their emotional wounds were slowly healing, and their time with one another was fun. The long weekend gave them an opportunity to spend some extended time with each other. Much of this time together was spent on the basics of day-to-day life. He helped with "handyman" type chores around her house, and they went grocery shopping together. One night, she cooked dinner. Activities like this helped to create a better picture of the real person.

Although the program had the full cooperation of the local authorities, it didn't want to have its team members conspicuously seen in these foreign locations. Additional steps were taken to mask the identity of the Americans as much as possible. Those without facial hair were instructed to grow it as well as letting their hair grow long.

Those with facial hair were instructed to let it grow longer. What minimal identification they were given was under assumed names. Scott, Joe, and Riley were given satellite telephones that required check-in every twelve hours or else the telephones would be disabled. The phones could also be remotely destroyed.

After the furlough, all members returned to Boulder for additional acclimation during which aftershave, toothpaste, deodorants, and anything else with a fragrance were banned. After this, they flew to a remote high-altitude airport in the country of Chad in northern Africa in unmarked military cargo planes. It was an uncomfortable introduction to the "real-world" part of the program.

TEN

Emi Koussi

Their trip made a stop for refueling at the former U.S. military base at Frankfort auf Rheine in Germany before flying to the small city of Bardai in northern Chad. Chad, in general, is a thinly settled country. Bardai is the major city in the Tibesti Mountain region, with a population of only fourteen hundred people. Its meaning in Arabic is "cold" because of the low nighttime temperatures that can occur there; in the winter months, it can drop below freezing. It's located one hundred miles east of the only north-south road that runs through the western half of Chad.

The Zougra Airport is a military air base located near Bardai and is closed to the general public. It has a single five-thousand-foot-long gravel runway. Soon after landing, they would begin the one-hundred-mile trip that would quickly rise as they approached the goal, Mount Emi Koussi.

Emi Koussi is in the southwest corner of the Tibesti Mountains and is the highest point in the Sahara. It's the tallest of what had been five volcanoes. Consideration was given to flying the equipment to the summit to shorten the length of time to make the swap, but it would have required multiple advanced technology helicopters that would have drawn too much attention, if they were even available. Chad having an average of two sandstorms per week was also a factor.

It was decided instead to make a small caravan of two transport trucks and two Land Rovers. Three days' transport in each direction with three days onsite was the plan. Each vehicle had a local driver. Two armed guards, both CIA-approved, were also provided for security. Joe was surprised to find that both armed guards looked like tiger children. He couldn't be sure because he had only seen them in the past for a few seconds at a time. They did look different from the other local people. It didn't appear they knew who Joe was. Since no one else on the Sixfold team knew the details of the Faneuil Hall shootout, and they were travelling under assumed names, no one looked surprised or otherwise concerned.

Scott had made all the local arrangements in advance, including food and local guides to assist in the climb up and down the mountains. He gave Joe his weapon of choice, a semi-automatic pistol, along with a silencer and one hundred rounds of ammo. For safety, Joe always concealed his weapon. There would be different teams for each hike as local people were needed as guides. All the local people wore a traditional headpiece wrapped around their head much like a giant scarf. When the wind and dust picked up, it could be raised to cover their entire face. The American team wore either unbranded baseball caps or the broader-rimmed Australian outback hat, more appropriate for this kind of terrain.

The trip to the mountaintop was slow, as there were no roads once you left the city. The ascent and slope weren't too steep, but they usually traveled across rock fields or loose sand. On occasion, all would have to get out of the vehicles and assist in freeing them up.

The view from Emi Koussi has been described as the loneliest place on earth. The landscape has been described as surreal, lunar, or Martian, and it goes on for what seems to be forever.

The scenery was as if it were taken from a Salvador Dali painting or Warner Brothers cartoon from the 1930s, with the winds having molded much of the sandstone into shapes defying gravity. Ancient black granite could be found in some places. Some of the rocks have been stained by minerals in the water and geothermal steam in the air and varied from shades of light tan to deep red. Nature had created a spectacular palette.

Although seven thousand years ago the region was lush and tropical, climate change had reduced it to little more than rock of various shades of bland. Now the weather is always hot, dry, and dusty. Radar scans of the desert floor showed evidence of large flowing rivers. Beneath this bleak landscape was a giant aquifer, a remnant from the former lush days. In its caves, early man drew paintings on the walls of crocodiles and lakes and many wild animals. Later paintings showed a drier climate and different families of animals and armies of men. By the time of 2,000 BC, desertification was well on its way.

Occasionally, there would be an oasis, a result of a rift in the aquifer lying below. The rivers that ran through its canyons disappeared in the desert sands before reaching the sea. The quick rise in altitude from the airport to the mountaintops made it difficult for the USA team to move around quickly, and the pace of everything had to slow down.

While the equipment was being worked on, Joe asked for a tour of the 'Top,' the crater of a monstrous prehistoric volcano. The crater was fifteen miles across versus a straight vertical ascent of hundreds of feet. The advance team had found a face on a wall that provided open viewing for the necessary fifteen hundred miles. Prior to leaving Colorado, Joe asked for and received refined satellite images of the mountains in question. He was dismayed to see an enormous deposit in the center of the crater that looked like a snow field but turned out to be natron.

Natron is a mixture of salts including table salt and bicarbonate of soda (baking soda). There was no way Joe could poke around and look for any hidden treasures in something so large or deep. It was certainly remote enough. Someone searching for the gold would have to know exactly where to go and have enough food and water not to mention camels to get there, retrieve it, and carry it back to civilization.

He was also looking for any evidence of rock coding, or "Chisel Coding," as they called it in the intelligence world. Rock can have any number of cracks and fissures in it and be moved by glaciers and sculpted by the winds. Cuts made in an otherwise clear and clean surface with no evidence of related stress or wear can indicate the presence of a code. The enormous area covered by the "Top" was too extensive for Joe to detect anything.

The installation and commissioning went smoothly, and the balance of the time onsite was uneventful. Clear desert skies allowed the locals to observe spectacular sunsets and sunrises in almost complete silence. They could also witness several celestial objects, including Shet Ahad (Pleiades), The Seven Sisters of the Night and Ursa Minor (The Little Dipper). Joe thought it was interesting how nomads could look skyward thousands of years ago and create images and stories from shining dots in the nighttime sky. For that matter, they could navigate as well.

Joe would quietly sit there and gaze out to eternity, thinking of his loves lost. Some of the music came back, but softly, due to the dangerous circumstances he felt he was in. He also questioned the coincidence of all that had happened to him in recent months. He left the CIA to leave the past behind him but somehow, here he was, back to where his problems began. Is it a coincidence or has someone or some organization been guiding these moves? Was his hiring at Pokey merely a "placeholder" to have him on board and available for these later events?

The trip back, beyond taking in the haunting scenery, was also uneventful. There was absolutely no way Joe could have quickly guessed where any gold or other valuables may have been hidden, and removing either would be difficult given who his guards were. They had a several-day layover in Bardai while equipment was loaded, and the planes were prepared for the next leg of the journey. The team was restricted to the airbase, and that was just as well. Nothing good could come of this team of six Americans wandering through this small city.

JEBEL MARRA

From Bardai, their cargo plane flew seven hundred and eighty miles southeast to a military airport near Al Fashir in western Sudan. From there, they would drive west to Jebel Marra. Joe remembered this site from his work in the region twelve years earlier. Jebel Marra is a monstrous and crumbling crescent-shaped mountain ridge on the west side of the Sudan in the region known as Darfur. Darfur has become infamous in recent years because of the civil war and related atrocities. Joe had his own nightmares. Foreigners didn't visit Darfur out of a fear of being kidnapped. In the bowl of the ridge was a large lake. Again, it appeared that two tiger children were their armed guards. This was now more than a coincidence.

Joe remembered Booka's description of them as being religious fanatics of sorts, and guardians of Musa's wealth, but why would they be interested in military installations in otherwise barren areas? That's unless they were among those looking for the gold and shared some of Joe's thoughts on where it might be hidden. It was interesting that they were on both high-altitude installations as part of the CIA "approved" team. Seven hundred years was plenty of time to infiltrate and corrupt the necessary organizations to ensure a local presence, should anything important be discovered.

Once again, the plan was to install and test the equipment in three days with two days of travel in each direction being part of the plan as well. This install would be a little better because it was replacing equipment installed years earlier by another team that included Joe. In this case, the equipment had been firmly placed on the face of a small cliff that could only be approached by someone who had the proper scaling gear and knew what they were looking for. It had to be positioned such that as much as possible was camouflaged with indigenous rock and anything that could be was protected by advanced Kevlar-type fabrics that could withstand the elements. After twelve years, they were still there.

The first night onsite was déjà vu for Joe. With the radar site to his left on the ridge and the lake straight ahead, Joe could close his eyes and mentally place where he saw scattered pieces of wood in the past, pieces that he thought strange given the barren moon-like terrain. They were located over the ridge several hundred yards from their camp. He wouldn't miss this opportunity to investigate them further and if still there, take a sample home, tiger children or not.

Morning comes early on rocky mountaintops. While the technicians were doing their work, Joe asked if he could take one of the Land Rovers and a driver to examine the general area, reminding him that part of his mission was to study the indigenous stones. Scott said okay and sent one of the security guards as well. They drove for several hours in the general area that Joe had remembered, stopping occasionally to look at a rock of some kind, take photos, and to pick up a few samples of soils and small and unique stones to take home for testing.

After two hours had passed, he saw what he was looking for. It was a flat piece of weather-beaten wood one foot by three feet in size and one inch thick. Judging from the way it looked, it could have been a tombstone or a marker of some kind, sticking slightly out of the ground. It obviously was a cut piece and not something pulled from a tree. Pressed into the wood were two rows of six stones, one on top of the other. The stones were about one inch in diameter, and evenly spaced in holes that had been cut into the wood. The placement of the wood, half-buried in the rock and difficult to access, was deliberate, not accidental. There were a few other weathered pieces that looked like broken two-by-fours partially buried in the soil. These pieces also had smaller stones pressed in them at regular intervals along their length. Someone had gone to the expense and time to bring them to the top of one of the most remote mountains in the world and place them there as indicators.

"I'm going to take a few pieces of wood for testing. They look like they may have been left here from a previous climb."

"I insist you leave them where they are; they may be religious artifacts," said the guard emphatically. He knew their presence had a greater but unknown meaning.

"If they were religious, they wouldn't be scattered about." It was a good try, but it didn't assuage the suspicious guard, who kept staring at the wood, even fixated on it.

The two of them gathered up the pieces of wood and put them in a sack in the back of the Land Rover and started the forty-minute ride back to camp. They were coldly cordial to each other, but the extended silences indicated that in both minds, the wheels were turning.

Back in camp, Joe showed the pieces of wood to Scott and said he intended to take them home for analysis. The guards were in a serious discussion in a non-Arabic dialect. The second guard asked to see the wood after which he too strongly demanded that it remain on the mountain. The two of them returned to their now heated discussion. They were highly suspicious of any unusual behavior, and Joe had no idea of what actions they might take as a result. He had to act.

He went back to his tent for a nap before dinner. He needed as much sleep as possible in advance of what would be a sleepless night. His discovery of the wood visibly disturbed the two guards. If they would take any deliberate action, it would be best to do it at night and claim that bandits had assaulted the team.

To prevent the removal of the wood, they had to kill Joe, but killing everyone would be very suspicious, especially if they returned to Al Fashir in good health. Their first action would be to kill the foreigner who was known to carry a weapon and trained to use it. As far as they knew, Joe and the technicians had no weapon, unlike Riley who brandished a sidearm, and Scott. He didn't know how to broach the subject with Scott without appearing to be a nut or exposing the whole gold theory. He did the best he could.

"I think the security guards we were given are a security risk. I think they are members of a radical group tied to preserving mountain holy sites. Their recent concern over my taking wood pieces for analysis and chattering between themselves has me worried. I'm afraid of an ambush as early as tonight."

"They have been vetted by our people. I looked at both resumes and spoke with both. They are clean; trust me." Scott didn't believe his worrywart friend.

"I disagree. I think they are sleepers, ready to take some aggressive action when required. We need to be prepared. Who has a cell or satellite phone?"

"Just you, me, and Riley."

"We need to keep close control of the three phones. Something's going on."

"Okay, I'll sleep with a loaded pistol under my pillow. Happy?" was a doubting Scott's reply.

Joe wasn't happy. Scott and Riley shared a tent as did Joe and the radar tech.

As the night progressed, Joe checked his pistol. He made a fake body for his sleeping bag with several dark face cloths, a poor substitution for his now long, flowing hair. He put his boots by the side of his sleeping bag and then slipped out of his tent into the rocks nearby and waited. And waited. Several hours passed before a slight movement caught his attention. It was one of the guards sneaking around Scott and Riley's tent and the other approaching his. It was too late to warn Scott or Riley.

Scott's tent was filled with gunshots. Joe quickly took out the first guard. Meanwhile, the second one had entered Joe's tent with the intent of murdering him. He was startled by the extra gunshots he heard, which were a different caliber from what they were using and muffled. He filled Joe's fake body with three shots before leaving the tent to meet Joe squarely in front of him. "Bye," was all Joe said while dropping him with two shots to the chest.

Sunrise was slow in arriving that morning, delayed by a cloud cover to the east. A bullet slightly wounded Scott, and Riley was dead. They broke radio silence and in code called for a medivac helicopter to airlift Scott and Riley to a hospital. The technical team finished their job and then hightailed it out of there and back to Al Fashir with the two security guard bodies in the back of a truck.

Joe and Scott spun the tale that the security guards and Riley had defended them against a bandit attack. Unfortunately, Riley and the guards were killed in the attack and the bandits retreated into the night. Joe and Scott didn't know how many bandits there were or if any of them had been injured or killed.

Thank God the project team had been prepared for such an emergency happening, and it was unfortunate that the fatalities happened. Joe didn't mention that he was carrying a gun. Scott was tended to and released, and Riley's body was flown home for burial. The remaining team would fly east and then south for two more installations.

Ras Dashen

Mount Ras Dashen is in the Semien mountain range in northern Ethiopia. It's the highest mountain in the horn of Africa. From its vantage point, most of the Middle East could be monitored. It's rocky and often covered with snow due to its high elevation.

The group flew eight hundred miles to the city of Gondar, located one hundred miles from the mountain. Unlike the previous two mountains, the airport is at an altitude of seven thousand feet and served by commercial traffic. The government required that they have armed guards to accompany them to just below the top of the mountain for security reasons.

Scott had found a replacement for their marine guard in one of the region's U.S. embassies. The marine was similarly tough and experienced in this area and type of covert assignment. The ascent here wasn't as difficult as the previous two mountains, and Land Rovers were enough to climb the gentle continuous incline. The major challenge was the presence of tourists. Unlike the remoteness of Emi Koussi, there were small villages nearby at high elevations and getting to the top was easy. The mountain itself is part of crumbling remains of what had been a giant volcano.

There was no way they could go to the top of the mountain without drawing much unwanted attention. The decision had been made to install the equipment on an outcropping much like Devil's Monument in Wyoming. Three days were set aside for installation and commissioning with a day of travel on each side as the earlier advance team had found and prepared the installation site.

Once again, two of the security guards were CIA-approved tiger children with the same overall appearances and, once again, between them, they spoke in a different language. They were closely watching all the activities. Joe made a point of memorizing and writing down two of their spoken sentences to have translated back at the base. Joe also asked the Ethiopians with whom he could converse either in English or in their local tongue if they knew these guards, or what language the guards were speaking. They did not. At no time on the mountain did Joe see any unusual pieces of wood or anything else of interest.

The job was completed with no delays, and the team returned to Gondar for a few days of rest while the next leg of the trip was being prepared. Since they had flown into a relatively unguarded commercial airport, the team was given permission to see the local sights provided they were accompanied by armed guards at all times. Scott and Joe were looking forward to this short R&R but were surprised upon their arrival.

"Uh, oh," said Joe to Scott as they walked toward the hangar.

"Exactly," was Scott's grudging reply.

A civilian meeting you with several military people at

their side was never a good sign in their world. This was no exception.

"Hello boys. I would like you to step into this jet for a short trip to meet with a few people who would like to speak with you."

Joe was in no mood for this. "Who the hell are you and where are you taking us?" he asked the mystery civilian.

"Someone important enough to have you handcuffed and dragged to the plane if my polite invitation isn't sufficient," was the blunt reply. "And you're going to Jizan." They realized this was a no-win situation for them and quietly walked over and climbed in the jet for an unscheduled meeting with unknown people and an unknown agenda.

JIZAN

Jizan is a large city located on the Red Sea in Saudi Arabia. Their one-hour flight, however, took them further inland to a secret military base that was also the home to several regional clandestine U.S. operations. Joe and Scott knew exactly what was up. The shootout on top of Jebel Marra had created waves in the spook world, and they were being called on the carpet to explain and defend their motives.

Upon landing, they were met at the airplane by a Saudi soldier who picked them up and brought them to a hangar which contained several nondescript offices. He was the last Saudi soldier they met. Someone else led them to a large conference room with tables and chairs, a large, clean whiteboard, and communications equipment to make secure conference calls. There were no flags or maps or anything else that could confirm the room's existence. Eventually, eight people entered the room with no one shaking hands. During the meeting, no one had names or ranks, but from their looks and demeanor, they were all Americans.

"Gentlemen, please have a seat," instructed the first interrogator. "Please explain to us firsthand what happened on top of Jebel Marra. Your brief report said that, as a result of an attempted robbery, three people were killed and one wounded. That's serious stuff. Now we find out that all the people killed were on our team. What's going on? There could be political repercussions to this, and we need to get to the bottom of this ASAP." The first interrogator was mean and lean, standing five feet ten inches tall and up-and-down trim. He wore desert khakis of American design and military boots, with a closely cut head of brown hair. His accent was American. He was probably in his mid-thirties and an officer of some ranking; he walked about doing his job without any concern or deference to the others in the room.

"It's as described in my report. The two guards tried to rob us and after shooting our American security guard and wounding me and trying to kill Joe, we took matters into our own hands. It's unfortunate, but that's what happened."

Interrogator number two was a bit chippy when he jumped in, "And what was it you thought they were trying to steal? The trucks? Your watches? Guys, you need to do better than that; these were experienced CIA operatives."

Interrogator number two was much younger and obviously trying to score points with his boss. At this point, Joe was a little tired and fed up with their bullshit. He decided to fight back and strongly.

"No, sir, you need to do some explaining. We have just finished parts of our mission in three different countries with three different ethnic groups speaking either Arabic or a local dialect, but for some reason, the CIA recruited the same foreign ethnic group for all three countries that, when no one was looking, would speak to each other in a very foreign dialect they suspected no one knew. I memorized two sentences that they spoke and checked with the internet on their meaning.

"They said, 'Are you watching them closely?' and 'Stay alert.' It was Aramaic. Why is the CIA recruiting this unknown ethnic group to handle a security detail in a series of Muslim countries? Why were they watching us and trying to kill us? Who instructed them to put their CIA contract in jeopardy? Where else have you used them where they may have cost us a mission or American lives?"

There was silence. Joe was on a roll and wasn't about to let up.

"If you don't believe me, look for yourself. Here is a photo of the Chad team. Here is a photo of the Ethiopian team, and here is a photo of the Sudan team. Look at these people. They are all from different tribes, but none of these security guards are local. Who is recruiting them? I'll bet on our next assignment, we get two more of these characters, too.

"I have a few more questions. Why are they the security

guards, and why did they go bonkers when I decided to save a few pieces of wood and some stones for analysis?"

"While you're at it, take a close look at who our guides are scheduled to be next week," said Scott, who was now emboldened by Joe's aggressive performance. "If I get there and find these same guys with us, I'm scrubbing the action, informing my superiors, and going home. We're not going to risk any more lives or the program until we find out who they work for and what their game is."

"Gentlemen, I think we have enough for today, thank you. No, we don't want to delay the program. We will make sure that proper changes are in place before you start next week's mission," was interrogator number one's assurance.

It was a quick visit. After a few more formalities, the same Saudi soldier escorted Scott and Joe back to the plane and soon thereafter flew back to Ethiopia, never knowing to whom they had been speaking.

MT. STANLEY

Imagine having a snowball fight in Africa! It's possible on Mount Stanley, until you're out of breath. Mount Stanley is located on the Uganda and Democratic Republic of the Congo border in the Rwenzori Mountains. Mansa Musa would have been aware of it because even in the fourth century BC, the Greeks were aware of it. Ptolemy called the range the "mountains of the moon." Europeans didn't climb it until 1906. It rises from the jungle to 17,000 feet in height, complete with glaciers. From its peak flow the initial waters that form the Nile River. It was the highest of the mountains they would be installing equipment on and the steepest and most dangerous to climb.

The team flew eight hundred and thirty miles south from Gondar to a military base just outside of Entebbe, Uganda, and drove for four and a half hours to the city of Ibanda, located at the base of the mountain. Ibanda sits at an altitude approaching five thousand feet. Its climate is classified as tropical-wet-savannah, unusual for a city so high in elevation.

Joe knew this would be a tough climb from his experience twelve years earlier as part of the secret team that placed radar equipment there as well. As a result, eight days were set aside for this part of the mission. Then, as now, top-level security arrangements had been made with the Ugandan government so that no one would be stopped or shaken down over a missing permit, etc. If necessary, the muzzle of a gun would be allowed to bring matters to a head and permit the team to move on with the program.

This would be a difficult and interesting installation for many reasons. First, its location was far south of where Musa would have hidden his gold on his return home from Mecca. He could have hidden gold or other valuables there later as part of a master plan. He might have needed to recruit a whole different set of guides given its southern location. Second, the climb here was very steep, hand over hand up granite walls. Unlike the earlier mountains, everything above a certain altitude would need to be done by foot on the backs of the team members, porters, or guides. At an altitude of seventeen thousand feet, the peak was now in the ultra-high zone, where people from low elevations couldn't handle either the lack of oxygen, or the cold temperature.

The mountaintop is usually enshrouded in cloud cover with mist, thunderstorms, lightning, sleet, and snow the usual weather. This was scenery straight from Hollywood... not encouraging for tourists but excellent cover for covert operations.

Due to the civil turmoil that had occurred in the region over the past century, there have been few hikers climbing it, no more than seventy per year. Just to be safe, the government provided them with twenty-five guards, guides, and drivers to work with and to protect them. Scott screened the guards; there were no tiger children.

The government had arranged for the team to have the exclusive use of several climbing huts during the mission that had been built and maintained by the Uganda Mountain Club. The day of the climb started in the rain forest at an altitude of five thousand feet. The climb quickly ascended in altitude, and their first stop was the John Matte hut at an elevation of nine thousand feet. An elevation of nine thousand feet is enough to slow down the walking of all but those who are normally acclimated to such an altitude.

The second day began in weather that was still temperate but cooling, much like you would experience while climbing almost any major mountain in the eastern United States. They quickly entered the Moss Forest. The daily dense mist that covers these and the plants at the higher altitudes allows them to grow quite thick and imposing. The moss was described by one early climber as looking like "leprous beards waving in the wind." The shapes of many seem to defy the laws of physics with shapes that appear impossible to structurally support.

Later in the day, they passed through the zone of giant Lobelia trees and cactus plants. Some of these plants grow over ten feet tall straight up, with towering spiked flowers on top. The best way to describe the landscapes they had just passed through was surreal with shapes and sizes that appeared to be on steroids. The same early climber noted in his diary that, "The vegetation seemed primeval, from a period of time when accepted forms and shapes hadn't yet been determined." They stopped for the day at the Bujuku hut at an elevation of thirteen thousand feet. Their timing was good as it had started to snow. Further adaptation to the thin air of this altitude was needed, and that extended to pace, rest, and food. At this altitude, there are no sounds other than your own.

The third and last hut was the Elana Hut at an elevation approaching fifteen thousand feet, or just two thousand feet below the summit. They wouldn't be going all the way to the top of the mountain because the advance team had already found a remotely accessible cliff area to place the sensitive equipment at a slightly lower altitude.

Prior to the trip, Joe had contacted NSA and asked for a specific scan of Mt. Stanley. He was pleased to find weak signals coming from the north side of the mountain, the area where the glaciers were still intact but melting on a regular basis. Joe spent the first day at the hut, acclimating himself to the altitude while the technical staff went about their business installing the equipment further on up the mountain. The second day with one armed guard accompanying him, Joe spent time at the edge of the glacier, blackened by ages of dust and pollution in the air. Anything now being exposed had been under ice for hundreds of years. In the back of his memory were exposed wooden boards one inch thick, two to four feet long, and three inches to one foot wide.

He never could figure out why anyone would carry them to this altitude unless they were to be used for shelter or firewood. Now he was sure they were used for signaling, but what? With much excitement, some of them were still there well-worn from hundreds of years of exposure and friction, along with more of the "two-by-fours!" All the two-by-fours had holes where stones had once been pressed into the wood. Most of the stones were gone. Some of the larger pieces of wood had the same two rows of stones while others did not. As with the smaller pieces, most of the stones were missing. Joe was intrigued enough to cut and record samples of all wood he found here and, for that matter, leading to the summit. Bringing them down would be far easier than bringing complete pieces. Given the nature of the project, no one asked any questions.

At the base of one piece of wood barely sticking out from under a series of flat stones, were what looked like several heavy pieces of bog. Each bale of muddied bog was eighteen by fifteen by six inches in dimensions and set side by side. It was as if they had been wrapped around something precious to keep it safe at over three miles in the sky.

Joe had no idea what was in these pods and could only hope their contents were valuable. He realized that the best he could do on this climb would be to bring only one pod down from the mountain. His dilemma now was how to get it out without drawing too much attention. It weighed over one hundred pounds and in this elevated altitude no one man could lift and carry it down the mountain. He had to gamble.

"Scott, come here," said Joe into his telephone. Joe felt that Scott was his only chance of getting such a large package loaded and down the high peak and on to a military airplane flying out of the country and then into a military base. Scott arrived five minutes later.

Joe spoke softly, "I think an ancient tribe used this tough environment to hide their treasures. They used special people to do all the work. I don't know what they did with these people after the work was through, but I'm sure very few people knew what was happening."

"Why the history lesson?"

"Because all of the tribes vanished hundreds and hundreds of years ago. There are no rightful owners. Once the riches are found, the local corrupt governments and militaries will take it all. See those pods of dried mud? I think they might be worth a lot of money, but I'm not sure. It's not practical or safe to open them up here. To lift one out of here is a two-man job. To get it into a truck without question will require positions of authority. It will have to be in a truck that's completely controlled. It will also have to be loaded into our plane with no interference by anyone and remain under our control at all times."

"Our control?"

"Yes, under our control. I'm offering you half of the

action, whatever it is, just to make sure we end up with its contents back in the States. You're the project leader, and I'm number two. If anyone asks, we're taking this pod-like thing back for evaluation. The fewer eyes, the better. You can play innocent all the way, saying I wanted to investigate the chemical makeup of this mud-like stuff."

"You know, it could also be a small body. That kind of action could throw us in jail. What do you think is wrapped up and how much are we talking about?"

"Yes, it could be the body of a child, which would cause problems, but why would a jungle tribesman climb over three miles into the air to bury a child with no appropriate clothing to do it? It's way too heavy for a small body. I think it's gold, several million dollars' worth. If you want more you can come back for it and hope no one else is looking. I'm out of it after this." It sounded crazy but risk free to Scott, so he agreed.

The two of them were able to lift out this piece of hardened clay and straw and, after knocking some of it off to make it easier to handle, brought it back to camp and put it in the back of Scott's bunk. When it came time to leave, they bundled it with lighter materials, trying to always mask its weight. At the base camp, they placed it in their Land Rover and the contents were dropped off at their accommodations at the fort.

With a weeklong stopover back in Bardai, they decided it best to see right now if they had indeed grabbed a large piece of gold or God forbid a small body. The answer came quickly. The pod was made of adobe like clay wrapped around a reed-like fabric that was held together quite strongly. It took a while to soak and cut through the baked-on dirt, and the many layers of wrap but eventually there it was a sheet of solid gold.

The best way to describe it was a sheet you would see in a candy shop, perhaps one-and one-half inches deep, nine inches wide, and fifteen inches long. But in this case, it wasn't fudge but pure gold! They didn't let their good fortune get ahead of them. They procured a large hot knife to cut the sheet into two closely equal pieces for transport out of there. So, to put the challenge into perspective, each man needed to hide a block of gold of approximate dimensions of one-and-one-half inches deep by four and a half inches wide by fifteen inches long. A kitchen scale weighed each piece at slightly over fifty pounds, worth over one million dollars.

Joe had only committed for the four installations, and Scott and the team had one more assignment, this time on the west coast of Africa, way down in Cameroon. Mount Cameroon had an altitude of 13,250 feet and was considered an active volcano. Joe was leaving to return home the same evening Scott's team was flying to Cameroon on what was only a scouting mission.

Joe had put his gold within the cover of a zippered research file of the same dimensions but titled, "Infectious Disease Results." It was now in the bottom of his carry-on luggage, along with his gun and ammunition. Since his were military flights, there would be no checking of luggage. He didn't know how or where Scott hid his money, nor did he care. Joe was hanging around just long enough to see first-hand who the CIA-approved guides would be for this mountain, which was nearly one thousand miles south of the usual trans-Sahara camel trains. He pointed out to Scott that they were again tiger children and wished him luck. It was no longer his problem. It was Christmas, and he was going home.

ELEVEN

Return to Hanscom

The official mission had been accomplished. One month later, all installations were still functioning as expected. Joe and the others returned to their regular jobs at Sixfold, a little tired for the effort, but otherwise in good shape and spirit. Several wanted to tell people about their journey, but fortunately were mature enough to realize it could lead them to the loss of a good-paying job and jail time. Joe was interested in seeing only two people, Sanjib and Nara. He had missed her during his time away.

Early upon his return, he slowly and discreetly sold the more than one million dollars in gold he'd brought home. Scott made it out of Cameroon with his health and gold intact. Scott's situation was different as he remained in the region under contract for a few more years. He was still working in the territory and unless careful, he could be subject to surveillance or retribution. Their plan was to keep in touch but through a sophisticated and timed routine to avoid detection.

Joe would regularly see Sanjib and share lunch or a drink after work. They kept in touch with Kevin, occasionally meeting with him at someone's home or at an out of the way bar to avoid suspicion. All they could get out of him was that the program had slowed down because of everything that had happened. The project had been granted a breather of sorts. Kevin's suggestion of an extension to document all the observations of the technical teams was accepted, and they were given six additional months to accomplish this task.

Joe tested the wood samples he had collected on the mountaintops they had climbed. They were found to be Albizia and Tali, both of which are known to fluoresce when exposed to ultraviolet light. Both are found in Africa with Albizia glowing a bright green and Tali glowing a bright yellow. The larger "tombstone-sized" pieces were made of one type of wood, but the smaller two-by-four pieces were made of multiple pieces of both woods pegged together. Some of the stones fluoresced, while others didn't. Taken together, they appeared to be part of a complex signaling system. They were signals to be sure, but what signals? Dig here? Left turn? No Smoking? It was likely that all the pieces of wood would need to have their surfaces cleaned and sanded to hopefully expose fresh chemicals that would allow the fluorescence to occur.

Joe wasn't sure how interested Nara would be in seeing him again since there had been complete silence during the last month of the mission in Africa. The first Saturday home, he took Nara to dinner and dancing on what was a semi-formal evening. He wore a suit and tie for the first time in many months. She wore a gown with one shoulder exposed and high-heel shoes. It was the raciest piece of clothing she had ever worn.

They had dressed up for the occasion at the Dexter House. This former mansion in the western suburb of Newton had been converted into an upscale restaurant. It had many small and quiet eating areas in what had been individual rooms, as well as a ballroom for after-dinner dancing to one of the region's best bands. It was expensive, but Joe had plenty of money to spend, especially given his recent overseas duty.

They did have some catching up to do. The evening went well and warmed as it progressed. The band and especially the lead singer were outstanding. Her sensual rendition of the Miracles *Do it Baby* early in the evening brought them into each other's arms. The slow dancing allowed them to hold each other close and gently squeeze. Her last song of the evening, Roberta Flack's *The First Time Ever I Saw Your Face* had them getting lost in the other's moistened eyes. Both needed some nurturing back to a fully functioning adult life. The feelings were still there.

One day, Joe stopped by Sanjib's office for a chat. After some small talk, he got right to the point. "I would like to get together with you to pick your brain on something, in private, where it's quiet. Maybe include Mah as well. It's personal."

"Okay, but if you want both of us, it needs to be after the kids have gone to bed. You could come over for dinner some night. What is it about?"

"Growing up Indian."

Two hours later, Sanjib called Joe to confirm the dinner date and time and per his wife's suggestion, they would invite Nara. She could offer an additional perspective and make the evening more pleasant.

FORREST

With the Christmas and New Year's holidays behind him, Joe decided to take some vacation time and, at his own expense, fly to Paris to once again visit the Musee d'Arabe. So much had happened since his last visit twelve months earlier. This time, he was on a personal mission. The weather was even colder than the previous year, but Joe was well prepared. With a scarf wrapped around his neck, a chapeau on his head, and fluency in French, he could have passed as a Parisian. The morning after arriving, he was off to the subway and a twenty-minute ride to the Musee. The Musee d'Arabe is in the Sixteenth Arrondissement toward the southwest part of the city. It's more of a residential neighborhood than commercial with the non-descript museum blending in with the district's apartment buildings and small shops.

A new receptionist greeted him that first morning and asked if there was anything she could help him with. She was young and of North African descent. He replied that his interests were the countries along the Sahel and any material that referenced the Mali kingdoms and Mansa Musa. She gave him some recommendations and offered to help him when the documents were in Arabic. Joe smiled and to her surprise, answered her in fluent Arabic that he could probably take care of that himself, but if he had trouble with some of the words or phrases, he would come looking for her. She smiled back and wished him luck. There was a little bit of flirting going on but also a showing of respect toward her language and culture by this handsome Frenchman.

Joe's plan was to spend three days in the Musee and hopefully, several hours with a different storyteller. He enjoyed his time with Mr. Booka the previous visit but felt he should compare and contrast his stories with someone else. He also wanted to squeeze in some sightseeing and visit one of Paris' major art museums. Joe promptly asked the receptionist if she could arrange for him to meet with a different storyteller on Friday morning. From there, he would leave straight away for the airport and return home.

The museum closed at five p.m. that second day, and Joe planned to return at nine the following morning to continue his research. He hailed a taxi rather than fight rush-hour subway traffic with his research folders in hand. It was his good fortune that a taxi showed up immediately.

"Hotel Essex," he said to the driver, who nodded and then quickly turned a corner to let another passenger join them for the ride. The driver remotely locked all the doors, and the second passenger immediately poked a small automatic pistol in Joe's side.

"Sit tight, be quiet. There's someone who wants to meet you," said the new passenger in a calm and soft voice in English. Joe thought, *an odd introduction, but I'm alive for at least a little while longer. They obviously know who I am because I spoke in French to the driver and everyone else that day*. A quick glance indicated the new passenger was of North African descent, same as the driver.

The heavy traffic was the usual rush hour for Paris. The driver brought them to the Fourth Arrondissement, which was historically Jewish. In a building whose primary tenant was a delicatessen, Joe and his new friend entered a foyer and quickly boarded an adjacent small elevator. The name over the elevator door was Timbuctoo Food Importers, Ltda. There was a guard as they entered and another as they exited. Whomever it was that wanted to meet Joe felt they needed a show of muscle every step of the way. As they exited on the third floor, went past a secretary, and entered a lavishly decorated office, Joe finally met his pursuer—a Chinaman.

"Hello Joe. We finally get to meet. How have you been?" said Joe's new friend with a broad smile and a short nod of the head, but no handshake.

"So far, so good. You tell me, how am I doing?"

"I think you're doing great. Welcome to Paris. Have you found everything you need?"

"Hmmm, no, not yet. I'm getting there but not yet."

"At least progress is being made. Have a seat. Can I offer you a drink?"

"I'll have whatever you have," replied Joe, with the slightest of grins.

"Excellent, and I'll let you choose which glass to pick up." As his host got up to order the drinks, Joe looked around the office. It had high ceilings as many old apartments and offices in Paris had. A fireplace was in the center of one wall of the room which had floor-to-ceiling windows facing the street.

"I don't believe we have met before, have we?" asked Joe.

"No, we haven't, but I know all about you. I feel like we grew up together in Syracuse. Spooky, isn't it? Oh, and my apologies for my team having tried to kill you several times... amateurs." Before Joe could ask the obvious question, the drinks arrived, brought by an aide.

"I could see the question die on your lips, so let me, if I may, complete it for you, as well as give the answer. Our African team tried to take you out on top of Jebel Marra. Our Boston team tried to take you out at Faneuil Hall. When the African job was bungled, it finally made it to my attention. I insisted they stop this foolishness and suggested a face-to-face meeting to see if we could come to a meeting of the minds. So, here we are."

Joe continued to be puzzled and asked, "Why all the trouble now to talk with me when in the past, you would have arranged an accident or faked a drug overdose or just killed me and thrown me in a ditch? And tell me again why you want to kill me?"

His yet to be identified host started speaking more forcefully, "First, let me clarify something. The professor was on our payroll but killed by the Russians, not us. Your spy girlfriend took care of that. She was indirectly on our payroll too. Secondly, I apologize for the thuggish approach my team has taken toward you and your friends and co-workers. Sometimes they get overly zealous about their responsibilities.

"Thirdly, I convinced my superiors that a man of your experience in international affairs is likely to have multiple copies of a document prepared and ready to be distributed to a government, a newspaper, a religion, several friends, and possibly in this day and age, private concerns, laying out in detail where they stand on 'commercial or philanthropic ventures.' We could kill you and then everything we're afraid of, everything we have fought to find or protect for seven hundred years, is on the front page of newspapers or the internet around the world, or just as bad, in the hands of a formidable competitor. You're worth much more alive than dead."

"You've been protecting or looking for some 'stuff' for seven hundred years? Are you the Knights Templar or something? Just what is it you're protecting? Gold? Diamonds? What are we talking about?"

"Mansa Musa's fortune. That's why you're here, isn't it? The gold and jewels are part of it, but most importantly, some of the world's most valuable real estate. How does a cool trillion dollars sound?"

"Aha, Mansa Musa. Now I understand. A trillion dollars, huh? So now we're chasing real estate? That should be cut and dry," replied a slightly sarcastic Joe, smacking his lips and rolling his eyes while looking around the room.

"You would think so. There are records of privately owned property in Europe dating back to the 1200s, far earlier in Japan. Some of it is layered through multiple layers of murky ownership. What do you think hundreds of acres of prime land in downtown London, Paris, Rome, and Tokyo would be worth?"

"Quite a lot, but Tokyo?"

"Yes, Tokyo. The king's people were trading as far east as Aden. Who do you think they were trading with, Jamaicans, mon? They were Indian, Chinese, and Japanese traders, offering spices, jewelry, and land. Four acres in Tokyo alone is a cool billion dollars today. We want what is ours, but we need the deeds. For hundreds of years, we have been chasing rumors, occasionally guessing on where the stuff is, but always coming up cold. Then you show up and out of nowhere, announce to the world that you know where it is and it's all going to the ladies of the world or else you're taking your ball and your bat and going home and taking the secret to your grave. Nice move; you almost succeeded!"

Joe was going into data overload with questions popping up in his brain faster than he could absorb the last statement. Whoever this guy was, he was excited by all of this. With a bit of a goofy look on his face, Joe leaned forward and slowly asked, "Who are you?"

"My apologies again, my name is Forrest Wang. My card." Forrest gave Joe his business card which blandly stated Forrest Wang –Food Industry Consultant. No address was listed, and the only contact information was a cell phone registered in Switzerland.

In Joe's extensive training, he learned to recognize and evaluate people's mannerisms and facial features. They could be manners, clothing, speech, grooming, tattoos, etc. Meeting Forrest over a Jewish delicatessen in Paris was strange enough. That aside, and forgetting his Swiss business card, Forrest spoke pure American English with no detectable accent or regional dialect.

As Joe would later see, Forrest's eating manners were pure American, opting to swap hands after cutting something and using the other hand to bring the food to his mouth. Proper European etiquette was always to maintain eating utensils in the same hands. Joe also noticed that the cut of Forrest's suit was American and not continental, as was his haircut and shoes. His suit appeared to be of top-quality material. Forrest could be a master of deception, but Joe would put money on him being an American of South China descent from the Rocky Mountain States, Hawaii, or the US west coast.

"Quite a big operation you have here," observed Joe, now relaxed and leaned back in his chair.

"It's not mine; I'm just a consultant, as the card says. I work for people, some of whom I've never met, but the money is good and the benefits terrific." After a short pause, Forrest bluntly asked, "So, Joe, where is the gold?"

This was all moving a little too fast for Joe. "You had mentioned a meeting of the minds. What did you have in mind? Why have you been telling me all of this?"

"It gets down to this. The current situation could be a win-win-win situation for all or a lose-lose-lose situation for all. We're willing to be pragmatic and practical in dividing the spoils if you will, but be sure, we will retain the over-whelming majority of what is rightly and historically ours. We know you have needs and your cause has needs, but let's also be realistic; a one-percent commission on a trillion-dollar deal buys all the cheeseburgers you could ever eat, give away, or throw away.

"Similarly, a larger but still reasonable donation to women's causes would far exceed anything that has ever been done in the world to date, especially if it could be leveraged with matching gifts from governments and private trusts. It would also be put into use ASAP. This accommodation we accept, but we do not accept forking over substantial amounts of our money to various governments which are in themselves corrupt and likely to have been created in the last ten to fifty years."

"Who is the third 'win' in the equation?"

"It's all of us; you, me, my superiors, women. It's that simple. Make it four or five wins if you like."

What Forrest was saying had some truth to it. His company, or whatever they were, had nurtured this situation for hundreds of years. What was a few hundred more years until they got exactly what they wanted? Money committed to women's causes today could be leveraged and provide the impetus for further actions, today, not in the next century.

Joe reflected on Forrest's comments for a bit and said, "Okay, so I understand the broad intent, which would need to be discussed in greater detail later. I'm not saying I agree with it, or accept it, but it is pragmatic and realistic. There's a parallel problem here that your Chinese management might not be aware of. The R&D project I've been assisting may unwittingly expose the answers to everything you're looking for to the U.S. government or whatever other foreign groups are developing the same technology or stealing the software."

"You mean project Pokey?" asked Forrest. "What a fucking name. It's either the work of a genius or an idiot. In any case, we're aware of the project and the fact, as you imply, spies are everywhere. By the way, my management is of African descent, not Chinese. Give them credit for recognizing talent regardless of race, religion, or sex. The Chinese, however, are among the suitors for the 'Pokey' technology, and we're watching them, too."

Joe said with a slight smile, "Well, we're not going to solve the problems of the world today. What is the next step?"

"Yes, there are a lot of things both sides need to work out. I'll be in Boston in eight weeks; let's plan on meeting then."

"What will you be doing there?"

"Attending a food conference. Read my card. Adieu; we can drop you off at your hotel or can call you a taxi. Your preference."

"I'll take you up on providing the ride, thank you." Joe thought any taxi they provided was theirs, so why fight it.

"Nice meeting you, Joe. See you in Bahstun." This time, Forrest's smile came with a handshake, and the taxi was his alone. Joe returned to his hotel that evening absolutely amazed by the just-finished meeting.

After more research on Wednesday morning, Joe spent the afternoon at the Musee d'Orsay, located alongside the Seine. This famous museum of nineteenth and early twentieth century art is in a renovated train station with all its opulence restored. This visit was followed by a quiet dinner for one in a small café near his hotel.

The receptionist at the Musee d'Arabe greeted him on Thursday morning with a serious look on her face instead of her usual smile. His appointment with a storyteller had been cancelled due to illness. She would do her best to find a replacement. Four hours later, she had to tell him she hadn't been able to make alternate arrangements on such short notice. She was very apologetic, and Joe was disappointed but didn't blame her. One hour later, she returned with a possible solution. She could arrange a meeting with a female agutta at nine a.m. the following morning, and the cost would be only thirty euros per hour. When Joe found out the reason for the low price was due to her not being a part of the storytelling guild, he said no thank you, not wanting to get anyone in trouble.

He changed his mind when he found out she was an old woman who was born and raised and spent most of her life living in Timbuctoo, the capital of the Mali Empire. To avoid suspicious eyes, the meeting would be held at a nearby coffee shop. Her name was Hawa.

Hawa was small and wore the traditional clothing expected of women in that part of the world. Outside of her clothing and around her neck was a necklace made of tumbled stones. Hawa is a rarely used Arabic and Malian name meaning Eve. Her face was wrinkled in a way that suggested she had spent most of her life outdoors in the sun. She could easily be eighty or more years of age. She was much more comfortable conversing in Arabic and was relieved to find Joe being fluent in it. Coffee and a plate of cookies were brought to the corner table they used. So began the day.

"Good morning, Miss Hawa. It's a pleasure to meet you," said Joe, smiling and extending his hand to his diminutive guest.

"Good morning, sir. It's nice to meet you. What can I do for you today?" Joe had given this meeting some advanced thought. In addition to wanting to meet with a different storyteller, he also came up with a different approach and a new set of questions.

"A friend of mine is writing a university thesis on the wealth of the Malian Empires. What were you told while growing up in Timbuctoo?"

She laughed and said, "That subject alone is good for several weeks of discussion. Can you narrow it down a bit?"

"Well, I've heard stories of incredible wealth, that gold grew like carrots, but it seems to have vanished. Is it still in Mali?"

"Oh my God, no," was Hawa's reply, with an embarrassing little snort. "We all heard those stories growing up. The university is still there, as are some of the old writings, so we know the kingdom existed and was wealthy and literate, but as for the fortune, it's gone, been gone for a long time, and hidden for many centuries now, thanks to Mansa Musa."

"You sound bitter, angry at him."

"No, it's not that. He had good reasons to hide it from evil and corrupt people, but he should have left clear instructions on how to find it! The people are still poor you know."

"What do you mean by 'clear' instructions? What

instructions were given? How do you know they weren't clear?"

"I don't know what the instructions were. There are various stories about there being six keys, seven, eight keys; it all depends on who's telling the story. The four elements and the stars in the sky seem to be woven into some of the clues, which can be convoluted and riddle-like. If the instructions were clear, someone would have found and spent the fortune."

"Okay. Let's change the subject; What is the Order of the Gazelle?"

Hawa's smile reminded Joe of Aziz Booka, slightly raising his eyebrows when Joe mentioned the same order to him a year earlier.

"The Order of the Gazelle was and still is a Christian sect dedicated to the Mansa. Its soldiers are the children of Dilla. They have some quite unusual physical features which has caused them ridicule over time. You can see them on occasion in some cities in the world, usually in the shadows. They were the guardians of his fortune, but now it appears they are like everyone else and looking for it."

"Have you seen them in Paris?"

"Of course."

"Why Dilla?"

"Probably because they could always be separated by religion, appearance, and called on to work at higher elevations. Remember, Dilla is a mountain city. Over time, boys from other cities were recruited but always high altitude."

"Were there any living in Timbuctoo while you lived there?"

"Yes, there were some."

"Did you ever see one of their weddings, or funerals?"

"Weddings yes, but funerals, I can't think of any."

"Don't you think that's odd?"

"Yes. Add it to the mysteries of the region."

"One of the riddles was that these children could see the sun and hear the wind, and there would be a pure light. This is all so much gobbledygook. We all can see the sun and hear the wind. What am I missing?"

"I think you have it a little mixed up. The true believers will see a pure light of the sun. A pure beam of a beautiful color or colors."

"Like what you would see with a rainbow?"

"You're thinking of the Irish, not Africans," said Hawa, and both had a good laugh. If anyone were watching them at that time, they would have assumed the conversation was anything but serious. "I think it will be a singular color, but who knows? Hearing the wind is more than the literal wind. It could be the drums of an enemy or the roar of a caravan or waterfall."

"Where should I go and who should I talk with to learn more?"

"There is only so much you can learn in Paris. You need to go to Mali and points along the Sahel. Talk to local aguttas and scholars. See with your own eyes what the aguttas are verbally describing and make your own interpretations."

"Where did you get that stone necklace, and why do you wear it?" asked a curious Joe.

"I received it from my mother who received it from her

mother and so on. I am supposed to wear it any time I am acting as an agutta. Consider it my badge, or permit." Hawa smiled.

The hour had passed quickly. Joe thanked Hawa for her time and excused himself to catch the metro for the airport and his flight home.

Thoughts on a Plane

The Delta Flight #57 bound for Boston left Charles De Gaulle airport right on schedule. Joe settled into his coach window seat and pondered the events of the past few days. There was so much going through his mind.

He felt an obligation to kill Pokey by whatever means he could. That wouldn't be easy since he had no knowledge of the software or hardware intricacies. He could cause physical damage, but that was it. Whatever the spies had already stolen was gone and being developed from their side. Speaking of spies, now he wondered who Forrest had on the inside, if anyone at all. Who else on the project was a spy, everyone? Skip's warning the first day of the project was spot on.

This whole series of events sounded like a sadistic spy-versus-spy-versus-spy parody from *Mad Magazine* with real people being killed in the process. Meeting with an eccentric Chinaman over a Jewish deli in Paris to discuss an African fortune which included Japanese real estate was a little over the top. After arranging for her boss to be murdered, Lexi shot and killed one of Forrest's guys and then got shot and killed herself by another of Forrest's guys, who was then shot and killed by a Boston cop. What had he gotten himself into?

He had to think about how to frame the agreement to fund women's causes in the region. How would it be executed and by whom? This shadowy group in Paris, or some organization back in the States?

He had to think about his own future, too. If Forrest had convinced his management that killing him was risky, as long as he was uncompromised, he was probably safe. If he accepted anything from them, however, they might be able to kill him off with no public relations or political issues. If he accepted nothing from them, however, that might affect his credibility.

Joe wanted to live a normal life. While a desk job would bore him to death, there was something nice about eventually coming home every night to a wife and kids and your own bed. If he decided to consult for Forrest, it could bring him in harm's way in any of the places he had visited in the past.

The flight began the long descent into Boston from over the Canadian border. On the few winter days like this when the weather was clear, the scenery was beautiful. Fishing village after fishing village would roll past his window with snow separating the land from the sea. In the distance, low level mountains covered in snow were silhouetted by the setting sun.

TWELVE

Growing Up Indian

The dinner at Sanjib's house was very pleasant. It wasn't quite the formal and extensive affair they had earlier for the broader office group but pleasant just the same. They were all curious and a little anxious about what Joe wanted to discuss. It could be something simple, but there had to be much more to it to ask for an "official" meeting.

"Mah and Nara, thank you for yet another great meal, and thank you and Sanjib for agreeing to meet with me. Things have been going through my mind that I can't get my arms around, and I need to have a better understanding of them."

"Okay, we all understand," said an expressionless Sanjib. "So, what is it you want to discuss?"

"You need to take your time and reach way back in your memories to come up with things you had long put away mentally. I need all of you to contribute. Sanjib, I'll start with you. What do you remember about growing up in India? Remember, this is a stream of consciousness."

Sanjib was a little annoyed. "Okay, I was quite small; I mean we moved to Africa when I was eight. In India, Ravi and I went to the local company-supported school; my dad had a good job with the steel company, so we had access to a lot of nice things that others didn't. We could see first-run movies. There was an employee-only bowling alley. We had good food, maid services. Is this what you want?"

"Not exactly but keep going. What do you remember about other people? Do you remember people of other religions, backgrounds? How often did you see white people or Chinese or black people?"

"Well. We had our dark-skinned Indians. I would occasionally see a European that had come for a visit and never a Chinaman. There were Muslims but few where we lived, and occasionally, someone of a weird sect. We saw mostly Hindus."

"Did you always feel safe?"

"Usually, if we were within the company compound or with our parents. You know, we were warned about going out at night or speaking with strangers and watching what we ate. There was generally little interaction with people outside of the company or family."

"What was it like when you moved to Africa?"

Sanjib paused a bit to reflect on the question. It was a long pause.

"It was quite different. I remember my parents calling Ravi and me into the kitchen on a Saturday morning. My mom said we had a big surprise. My dad said we were going on a long adventure, to Africa. We would get to see new animals and different places. They tried to make it sound exciting, but Ravi and I cried because we would miss our grandparents and school friends. We spent most of the time in Addis Ababa and a year in Khartoum. We did get to travel about with our parents to see some of the remote cities. On vacations, we did get to several wildlife reserves and see unusual animals. We were different though. We were different-looking foreigners, and rich by their standards. The locals resented this, even though we were dark like them. There was the occasional Indian family, but they were local merchants who had emigrated earlier."

"Okay, now you're in Africa and the same questions as before. Did you run into any Europeans, Chinese, Muslims, Christians, fanatics?"

"In general, it was the same story as before, as long as we were in the compound. Once we left the compound, things were quite different. Now we were seeing real blacks, and many of them, along with many Arabs. We saw few Europeans or Asians, some Hindus."

"You didn't answer my question about religions. Could you separate out Christians, Jews, and Muslims?"

"We knew who they all were, but we were kids and didn't pay too much attention to them, nor did we care. Where are you going with this questioning?"

"I'm trying to take you to a point in your memory where you'll open up. Exactly where did you first run into the tiger children?"

Sanjib was now very animated, "Those bastards! When Dad was looking for new mineral deposits, he and Mom would occasionally bring Ravi and me with them if it was someplace we had never seen before."

"Where were these areas?"

"Usually in the highlands where the minerals would start to occur."

"At what elevations and in what countries?"

"We would usually be at altitudes higher than one mile because I remember Dad having trouble breathing. It could be anywhere in northeast Africa—Chad, Sudan, Ethiopia, Kenya."

"What would they do to you?"

"They would harass my parents and us kids. 'Go away, infidels' or some crap like that. They thought we were going to steal their ancestors' spirits or bones or something. If they could, they would circle around Ravi and me and make weird noises in weird languages."

"Did they ever speak to you in Hindi or English, or Arabic?"

"It was a language none of us understood, which included all three of those. Someone would translate for us."

"Did you ever run into them at lower elevations or by the sea?"

"Never."

Joe was now digging for details, "Tell me what they looked like... height, weight, color, facial features. How many of them were taller than you? How many of them were your parents' age or older? Were they tough looking? Do you think you would win a fight?"

"They looked like the guys we saw in Somerville and Boston. I was taller than all of them, and I'm five foot eight inches tall. They all were younger than my parents—teenagers or ten years older than me. Twenty-somethings.

No gray-haired elders. Regarding a fight, I could have beat half of them. They were short and some were stocky, like small rugby players."

"Were there any women with them?"

"Yes, some, and they were small too. They kept their distance."

"Were they covered up head to toe?"

"No, they weren't."

"Okay, then they were Christian, Jew, Hindu, or a local sect."

"They weren't Hindu, because we would have recognized them and their language."

"Did their leaders wear any kind of identifying jewelry like a cross or Star of David or something else?"

"I don't remember."

"Okay, I have one last question. Why do you call them 'tiger children?' There aren't any tigers in Africa. They are native to India."

"I don't know why, unless it was an Indian, you know like my parents, who used the best description they could that I could relate to. They probably had another name, more local."

"Thanks," said Joe and turning to Nara, asked, "What do you remember about growing up in the region?"

"Unlike Sanjib, I was raised completely in the region. I never met little people like Sanjib described, but then I never went out and up into the highlands. I do remember, however, being aware of the various power brokers wherever we lived. My parents, being of mixed ethnic groups, were always sensitive to the political winds. You had to be aware of where the power brokers stood on every issue, and not make waves."

Joe smiled and said, "Thank you, Nara. Mah, what do you remember?"

"I'm afraid I remember little. I wasn't only young but very insulated by my family. I didn't see any of these characters."

"Okay, thank you all for sharing your memories with me; you've been very helpful."

Sanjib posed a question to Joe, "Now that we're finished talking, it is your turn. Based on what we have just told you and you've already discovered, what are your subsequent findings?"

"I haven't finished gathering my thoughts, but when I do, I'll be happy to come back over and share them with you."

"In exchange for another free meal," quipped Sanjib.

KILLING POKEY

It was another tough evening of "reflection" in Joe's apartment. In the distance, a thunderstorm passed behind the Boston skyscrapers and with the preceding lightning, adding to an already tense situation. Joe sat, drink in hand, looking out to space for an answer to what to do about Pokey. Pokey had several nice attributes to it, but also several major faults that could destroy civilization. The first was falling into enemy hands to be exploited for future military use. The second was more sinister. If by virtue of developing the advanced software and hardware for the military high-speed sensor recognitions, the location of every living person could be easily tracked and monitored. The frequency of every living person who ever lived could possibly be mapped, and their persona displayed on a computer monitor.

Finding Musa's frequency and locations of his vast wealth would eventually occur by trial and error. This was secondary. Life on Earth would change dramatically and become a freak show with every existing belief, be it personal, religious, historical, sports, you name it, available to review for a fee on the internet or in social media. Everyone, every emotion, every fear, and everything would have a price. To survive this potential continuous challenge of your beliefs and feelings, many people could forego the pleasures, wonders, and uncertainties of life and become inert. If it were controlled by one country or religion or company or one person, they would become the king of the world.

What little Sanjib and Joe were hearing about the project was that things had been moving slowly since the shooting with the required training of replacement people, increases in security, and other things. The point is, things were moving forward. Unless Pokey was stopped or seriously delayed, it was a matter of a few years before all the dots were connected and the games for control of the world began. Life had its ups and downs before Pokey but in general, life was good. Pokey's downside far outweighed the upside. Joe felt strong moral and ethical reasons to act. Pokey must die.

A few things needed to be done. Could either Joe or

Sanjib or both get back into the program? Had enough time passed so that inquiring media and third-party eyes wouldn't notice? Could Joe get involved again from the other side through Forrest? Chances are good that someone in the program is leaking info to external interested parties; it always happens. From the USA position, this was undesirable because it meant someone else would not only be in the same race but ahead of us.

From Joe's perspective, he wanted to derail the whole thing. If Sanjib could get involved again, he would have access to the development, and a far more interesting job than now. They started their campaign with Skip, inviting him to lunch at a Chinese restaurant named the Laughing Crab located halfway between Bedford and Cambridge. Its lunchtime buffet was well known in the area, and there was often a line to get in. They greeted Skip at the door with smiles and handshakes.

"Nice to see you again, Skip. How have you been doing?" asked Joe.

Sanjib joined the conversation, "Yeah, Skip, how is it going?"

"Boys, it's nice to see you again after all of these months," said a smiling Skip. "I hope you're keeping busy out there at suburban Hanscom. From what I remember, it isn't a fun place to work."

The hostess guided them to a table where their first action was to order tea and the buffet lunch.

"It's kind of boring to be honest," replied a somber Joe. "Skip, we miss being on the team. We can't ask you specifics on how the program is progressing, but we can see that it would move faster if both of us were reinstated. It has been awhile since the Faneuil Hall incident. In my case, I've been in the geographic area of concern in recent months on behalf of the Hanscom company I work for, updating much of what was believed to exist. Current info would be far more valuable than historical and add that to whatever else I had for an edge over my replacement."

After a first pass at the buffet line, they sat down and ate. "Joe, you weren't replaced, at least not yet," said Skip, moving from wonton soup to crab rangoon and egg rolls. "A person of your elaborate training does not come along every three months, let alone every year. It's still open. Filling the position would also be a matter of economics."

"Skip, what about me?" asked Sanjib.

"They may be interested in you as well. They need to make up a lot of time. I know they have been talking about the two of you, so maybe the timing is good."

After a good and filling lunch topped off with lychee nuts and pineapple slices, they shook hands in the parking lot and went back to their respective jobs for the balance of the afternoon. Skip said he would make a few telephone calls on their behalf and get back to them.

The following week, Skip called each of them with the same message, "They are interested in talking with both of you about rejoining the team, and they will be here in three days at ten a.m. at the FBI office in Boston. The first general meeting will begin at ten and then break into smaller groups as required. I expect the FBI, CIA, and NSA people to also be present." Sanjib and Joe looked forward to an interesting day.

The FBI office in Boston is in the Tip O'Neill office building in Government Center, in the downtown area with a view of the Quincy Market and Faneuil Hall. Skip was correct in that there was a crowd ready to meet with the men in a large conference room.

"Thanks for joining us today, men," said the lead FBI agent. "It has certainly been a challenging nine months since the incident at Faneuil Hall. While much has changed, much hasn't, and we need to get our arms around some of the events and what they meant and mean going forward. One of the issues the leadership continues to ask about is what happened at Faneuil Hall and why?

"We still haven't found out who the potential assassins were, who they were working for, and where they were from. Heck, we don't even know if there are more of them. For today, we want to break into two groups with Skip, and the NSA team, bringing Sanjib up to speed on Pokey, and the rest of us will meet with Joe to discuss what happened on his recent trip to Africa. After that, we will break for lunch, and that will be it for the day. You boys can report to work Monday morning. Got it? Great, let's go. Welcome back."

With the group now reduced to Joe, the FBI, the CIA, and one person from the NSA, the discussions began again, this time having moved to a smaller office. Joe didn't recognize any of them as having grilled him before, but they still filled the obnoxious personas and general descriptions of the people he met in the past.

"Joe, we have a bunch of things to discuss with you. Let's start with your recent road trip through Africa. How did it go?" asked the CIA lead, hands folded across his chest while leaning against a table.

Joe was put off by the tone of the question. Either they were using his return to "fish" on behalf of others, to poke holes in his story, or the intelligence agencies weren't talking to each other. He replied sarcastically, "Well, the in-flight food was horrible; I'm not sure it was all dead. The pillows were rolled newspapers, I mean, can you believe…"

The CIA lead jumped back in, "Cut the shit, Joe. The specifics of decommissioning and installing new listening equipment bore all of us to death. We're not interested in the menu or if you were comfortable either. The specifics of the trip's issues are what we're interested in, so get to the point." This tone had Joe even more sarcastic and worked up.

"Okay, so we fly to Camel Dung, Chad, a small city where ninety-nine percent of the people are a local tribe but somehow our security detail for the trip to the mountain were people who looked like the two gunman who were killed down the street from here. Then we fly back to camp and reload our plane and fly off in another direction for six hundred miles to another base and another ethnic group in Sudan and guess what, two more of these strange-looking people who again don't look like the locals nor speak like the locals are the security detail. I caught them speaking Aramaic. The same happened later when we flew nine hundred miles to Ethiopia.

"That's where I picked up some stones and pieces of wood scraps that looked like they had been carried up the mountain for a building. These guys went crazy over that, and I pointed that out to the project manager. When they shot and killed our American guard, the project manager was able to quickly respond and only suffer a grazing himself. I was waiting for my killer to enter the tent and just blew him away when he arrived.

"We were able to make sure they weren't on the climb in Uganda. I took off to the airport and flew home. Mission accomplished."

"What about the dead bodies?" asked the NSA agent.

"We deliberately didn't phone in anything, not knowing what else may be waiting for us back at the base, or in Uganda. Our American guard's body was flown home, and the two guards were, well, I guess I don't know what happened to them. You tell me."

"Their bodies were picked up by a company we've used for years for clandestine missions like this. We don't know who owns this company but need to check because they're used throughout northern Africa and into parts of the Middle East. They claim they gave the bodies to a church for burial," was the CIA response.

"And in the USA?"

"We haven't seen them since the shootout," replied the FBI lead agent.

"That's not what I meant. Who picked up the bodies in Boston?"

"Initially, no one. After two weeks, we contacted a local Eastern Christian church, because one of the guys was wearing a cross. They took the responsibility of giving them a proper and local burial."

"Did you tape the pickup? Did the people look like them? Were they black?"

"Yes, we videotaped it and yes, they were black but of east or north African descent, most likely Arabic, but completely normal people and part of the local community for many years."

The NSA agent spoke up, "So, Joe, here is what we have. We're working on what is now a highly secret project that could affect our national security. We expect our major competitors to be snooping around as well as our friends. In pursuing this project, we have somehow brought in what appears to be an African secret religious group whom we have upset.

"On the surface, we upset them because you had this big meeting down the street to say you know where all the loose gold is in Africa, and you're only going to spend it on women. Then you find some sticks and stones they thought were 'special' and so pissed them off they tried to kill you and the team leader. What are the common threads? It looks like it's you, them, and the gold." Joe thought, *where do they find assholes like this?* He was tired of being grilled by desk jockeys. He was still angry and had more questions.

"There are side issues, gentlemen, like why were they already in Boston with weapons before I made my announcement? How does a secret group like this get CIA contracts for clandestine operations at least in Africa, and elsewhere? We also have Pokey—are they interested in that? If not, why are they in Boston and not Cleveland or St. Louis or New Orleans?" He realized he had made a mistake mentioning the wood earlier and deliberately avoided bringing up the wood again.

The NSA lead recognized this discussion was going nowhere. He paused and said, "There are still a lot of open issues. We need to get together on a regular basis to work them through, one by one. For now, Joe, welcome back to the team. We will arrange a meeting with you in the next three to four weeks to discuss this further. Let's have lunch."

NAHANT

Joe expected his follow-up meeting with Forrest to occur in the same manner as the first; someone kidnaps him and drives him to a nondescript place like an office over a Chinese restaurant or strip club in Boston's combat zone. Not this time. He received a call.

"Hello, Joe, it's Forrest. How are you?"

"I'm fine, thanks. Where are you?"

"I'm here in Boston on business for a few days. How about getting together for a beer and maybe dinner?"

"Sounds good. When and where?"

"Well, I tell you my schedule is pretty full. I'm going to be on the North Shore the next two days. How about coming up here, say tomorrow night, five p.m.?"

"Sounds okay. Are you going to pick me up?"

"No, I wasn't planning on it. Boston, it's your home. Do you have a car? The driving is easy, I'm in Nahant. Do you know where it is? If not, I'll give you directions."

"No problem, I know where it is, but go ahead with street directions."

"Great. Drive to the very end of Nahant. That's it. That's all you need to know. See you at five."

Forrest wasn't kidding. The directions were simple. Nahant was a peninsula sticking off the north shore of Boston. Most of the cities and towns on the North Shore had extremely expensive properties along the coast, and Nahant was no exception. At one time, it had been a summer resort for Boston's wealthier families. The very end of the peninsula with the most spectacular views had been appropriated by the U.S. military during both world wars as spotting locations for German U-boats. Huge cannons were built into embankments in several areas here and on the southern approach to Boston Harbor. Anything that passed through the two harbor entrances could be blown out of the water very quickly.

Behind what used to be a nightclub along the shore, one can still see the concrete casing in which the monstrous fifteen-inch guns would operate. Closer to the center of town are stairways that go under the street to a secure underground military site somewhere in the area.

Joe drove through the little seaside town past several beautiful homes and a beach called Forty Steps. Once he came to the end of the road, past several of the remaining World War II observation towers, he knew he had arrived. A guard opened the mansion gate for him, and another escorted him to a waiting Forrest, who sat at a table on the front lawn and nursing a drink, courtesy of a warm and sunny spring day. He wore a blue blazer, should the wind pick up. The front lawn of the home rolled down to the ocean and had a stupendous view looking out at the Boston skyline.

"Joe, nice to see you again. Welcome!"

"Hi, Forrest. Nice place you have here. You find it on the internet?"

"No, it's actually a Marriott timeshare." Seeing the look on Joe's face, Forrest chimed back in, "Gotcha! It belongs to an acquaintance. I'm here for a couple of days. Will you have a beer or wine?"

"White wine, please."

"Excellent!" Forrest turned and placed their order with an aide and then addressed Joe. "So, it has been eight weeks since we met. What do you think?"

"I think we can work together as we have overlapping mutual interests. It will be, however, a different relationship."

"Intriguing; tell me more."

"You can keep your gold and property. My major concerns are the improvement in the welfare of the region's women, and the destruction of project Pokey, and a little something for myself."

"Your humility is commendable, if also stupid, but it's your choice. Why so much animosity toward the Pokey project?"

"If I guess where I think the project may unwittingly wind up, it will end modern civilization as it exists today."

This caused Forrest to go, "Hmmm. Maybe I should use up my frequent flier miles quickly. Why this unbridled love for the women of the world and fear for the end?"

Joe, after a long pause, replied, "It's because of what I've seen."

Appetizers and salad were brought to the table. Forrest paused for thirty seconds while eating a shrimp then dryly asked Joe, "Might you be exaggerating just a wee bit?"

"Not at all. The race is already between you and others to find the riches before the results of Pokey blow it wide open for everyone. After that, so goes civilization. Its hardware and software are so advanced that...."

"I don't need the details. So, you're saying we had better get moving. What do you propose?"

Joe had given this topic a lot of thought in the past eight weeks. He figured he'd ask for "the moon" while he had a negotiating chip to play. He didn't know how much money was out there to be found. He also didn't know what life would hold for him as a result of being involved with Forrest and his effort.

"I'll begin passing you information on where I think gold is hidden. No strings attached, all verbal and handshake, little in writing. Please note I don't intend to visit these places; been there, done that with most of them. What I expect from you is a commitment to quickly sabotage the Pokey project and create a substantially funded foundation set up in advance to assist the women of the region. The foundation will be replenished by forty percent of whatever is found of Musa's fortune. My commission will be five percent."

"It ain't gonna happen, Joe. No one will accept that amount."

"Then the fortune can stay where it is for another seven hundred years."

"By your own calculation, that's not going to happen either. I don't know what your idea of 'sabotage' is but these days, everything important is backed up somewhere. Pokey will eventually expose it in what, three to five years? Then what? Your ladies won't have a dime, and you'll still be eating takeout. We will, however, accept to pay a ten-percent commission to the foundation or you on the assets recovered as a result of your efforts. You can split it up anyway you want; we don't care. We feel that's fair. That's as much as one hundred billion dollars, which could grow with matching gifts from various foundations around the world."

Joe was quiet and thinking. Forrest's management could wait another century without "blinking." A successful Pokey could make all this moot. Some money is better than no money, and in this case, "some money" was an incredible amount that needed to be put to work now to correct inequalities that would take decades if not generations to cure. Mentally, he figured on keeping one half to one percent for himself, but he wouldn't tell that to Forrest now. It may work to his benefit to appear to be greedier to Forrest.

"Okay, I accept your offer. We will decide on the splits and how and where they are to be paid later. Let's move on."

"Great. When will we start seeing where the gold is?"

"I have a list of some of the locations where I think it has been hidden."

"Did you bring it?" asked Forrest with just a slight indication of anticipation in his voice and widening of his eyes.

"Nope, it's in my desk at work. I'll give it to you the next time we get together."

"Fine. Regarding the sabotage, what are your thoughts there?"

"The two areas are the software and the hardware. Whatever has already been stolen may be undergoing further development on the other sides. That's out of our control. The hardware is constantly being updated in the facility. The software is my biggest concern."

"It's probably best to introduce a worm into the software and let it run for a while to be sure that others who are chasing the project are also infected. I'll take care of that."

"You will?"

"Yes, I will. Just be sure to allow some time to pass between my work and yours, like two to three months."

"Okay then. I'll take care of the physical destruction of the facility. That will set them back for a while, as well as wipe out any of your fingerprints on the hardware. I suggest we do this on the Fourth of July, which gives us three months to prepare."

"Should be doable. You're okay with explosives? Of course, you are. I forgot your background. Okay, let us plan to get together again in two months' time for one final review."

The sun was going down and the evening cooling off, so they moved inside to finish dinner and enjoy a cordial. After that, they shook hands and bade one another farewell for the evening. As Joe drove back to his apartment, he hoped

Forrest had taken the bait. Instant access to the location of the troves of gold could prove too tempting for Forrest to resist and instruct his project mole to access them as soon as possible.

Joe hoped that his interloper, while rummaging through his desk, wouldn't notice the micro-cam hidden on the shelf among the various knick-knacks, sending images of everything going on to Joe's home computer. By eight the following morning, Joe had caught his fish.

THE MOLE

Skip, thought Joe. Joe couldn't believe his eyes. There, courtesy of his hidden camera and caught on screen, was his boss rummaging through the papers on his desk and using his master key to open the drawers to Joe's desk and poking around there as well. The bait had worked and actually had some value. On a piece of paper, Joe had listed ten of the highest mountain sites in Africa, including one in the Azores and others in Kenya. All were at least ten thousand feet in elevation. They were real candidates, so no harm was done, nor suspicions raised. Later that Monday afternoon, Joe quietly removed his camera from the shelf.

Skip must be a desperate man but having suffered a bitter divorce, who knew what his financial and emotional status was. From this action, Joe assumed that Skip would put the software bug in the system and let it do its thing.

Joe also was surprised by an announcement he saw on the internet the following week, announcing the creation of an anonymously funded Saudi-based foundation for the "well-being" of women in the region. No mention was made of the amount of the funding. Forrest appeared to have quickly kept his part of the bargain. Now, it was up to Joe. He had to perfect a plan to destroy the physical evidence, convince Nara to marry him, and start a new life somewhere else. "Easy peasy!"

The project continued with improvements being made regularly and reported on during Skip's monthly meetings.

"Okay, people, let's get going. I've got a busy day. The two new programmers were brought on board last week. Sanjib, how are they doing?"

"So far so good. Both are showing up on time and putting in a full workday. It's obvious both have the experience they claim to have, so I expect they will work out well. It was another good month for code writing."

"Good. Kevin, what about your new hardware engineer?"

"She is doing okay, Skip. Like Sanjib's team, she works hard and knows her stuff. Unlike them, however, she is new to the area and is having a problem finding a place to live at a reasonable price."

"Welcome to Boston," snorted Skip. "Joe, anything new on the regional geology?"

"Yes, and I'll have it and an update on the effects of weather on signal transmission in a PowerPoint presentation for the next meeting."

"Okay. Kevin."

"Well, okay, we continue to introduce upgrades into the system. Our problem is in quality control. Per your instructions, we have been pushing the limits as far as we can. The problem in doing this is that we get ever increasing speeds, but we're not getting the corresponding repeatability. We've checked with the utility, and it's not them. The recently installed air conditioning equipment has helped some. It's great that we're moving forward, but at some point, we need to introduce repeatability into the system. Sanjib will talk more about this. Sanjib?"

"Yes, it's as Kevin says. We're always dealing with a moving target. We're having some issues with wave repeatability, both sine and square wave. On top of that, we keep getting what appears to be dust or lines or squiggles on the screen. The higher the frequency, the more we see. At some point, we need to fix the frequencies and fix the problems or else we may continue to look at dots and squiggles and such forever."

"Keep at it. If there's nothing else, meeting adjourned."

Nara's Evaluation

Nara and Joe were spending much more time with each other now. She found Joe to be intriguing and athletic. He was handsome and in great physical shape and good fun for all kinds of activities. He was warm and tender, attributes she needed. He needed someone like that, too. There were days when his job would have him all worked up, and she could bring him back to earth. He was sensitive and caring, too. They would occasionally meet with Sanjib's family, and she noticed that Joe liked to play with Sanjib's kids, and they with him. Kids and dogs were good judges of character, and they all gave him a paw or thumbs up. One evening after dinner at Sanjib's and after the kids had gone to bed, Nara thought to ask him about this.

"Well, you always spend a lot of time playing with Yogesh and Anika. They must really like you."

"Yeah, they are a lot of fun. I like kids. Maybe I'll get married someday and have a few of my own."

"That's a team effort, you know. How many kids do you want?"

"I would like somewhere between four and six. Who knows? That will depend on my wife."

"Well, then on behalf of your future wife, thank you. I would like kids also someday." That was obvious to Joe as he could see how much she loved her niece and nephew.

Joe said, "Let's have a talk tonight after we go home."

THIRTEEN

The Trailers

The next meeting Joe and Sanjib had with the FBI team was held four weeks later in one of their field office trailers.

"Boys, now that you're back on the Pokey project, we're going to place both of you under constant FBI surveillance. It's to protect you and the project, and to determine if any more of those gunmen have been assigned to Boston, either as replacements for the two you killed off or as a larger group," said the lead agent. "We're going to assign more people in the greater Boston area to keep a lookout for them in academic and R&D circles.

"Thanks a lot, guys," was Sanjib's reply, slightly shaking his head as he said it. "By the way, we didn't kill them. A Russian spy and a Boston policeman did."

"You're right. Anyway, the plan is simple, live life as usual. You're back on the program and that should interest them, if they're still here."

Joe interrupted the agent and said, "Excuse me for just a minute, but as I remember, they tried to kill both of us, me for intending to expose their gold, and Sanjib for trying to rescue me. They are fanatics; what is to stop them from killing us as we walk out of this building today? Are you trying to tell us you haven't seen any of them since the incident in Faneuil Hall? That has been awhile. Since a bunch of them had CIA clearance, what is to stop them from killing us in this building?"

"What do you mean they have CIA clearance?" asked a surprised Sanjib.

"Shit. Sanjib, not here but in Africa," replied Joe. "How are we to know they don't have it here as well?"

The lead agent replied, "Look, we haven't seen any more of them since the incident. Let's see if anyone shows up."

Sanjib and Joe left the meeting and went for a cup of coffee. After a minute or two of silence, Sanjib started the conversation, "I hadn't given the tiger boys a thought at all since the event. I had been living life as usual with no fear, and now they tell us to go out to see if we can draw any of these guys out from hiding. Are they kidding?"

"I don't get it either," said Joe. "Up to now, the FBI has been invisible. For all we know, they have been watching us all along; who knows? They didn't ask us to be more observant or call them with any observations or fears. I'm guessing they wanted to tip us off that they will be watching us and may show up somewhere or sometime unexpectedly and didn't want us to be surprised. Or, they may be just covering their asses. I doubt if they will watch us that closely; that's too Hollywood."

Coffee finished, they went back to work. Joe remembered Forrest's statement saying he was worth far more alive than dead, but he wasn't convinced that message had worked its way through the organization. It was possible that there were other assassins after him, too.

Several nights later, they went to a new place after work for a couple of beers with Kevin. They got there late and found a parking space in the back of the adjacent lot.

Dinner and several drinks later, they left the building and were close to their cars when two men of average size and wearing black clothes jumped out from behind another car, brandishing knives and demanding their wallets. Kevin was immediately upset, but Joe and Sanjib remained calm and shook their heads because they thought it was an FBI setup.

"Wallets now and no one gets hurt. Now!" demanded robber number one in a hushed voice, waving his knife around as if he would initiate a thrust move with a sword.

Kevin threw his over immediately but with smirks on their faces, Sanjib and Joe stood their ground.

"Isn't this a little soon and obvious, guys?" said Sanjib loudly.

"Who are you talking to, man? Give me your wallet," demanded the first robber.

"No, I won't," said a defiant and loud Sanjib, making a face back at the robber. "What are you going to do about it?"

The robber was taken aback with his brazenness and loudly shouted, "Your wallet, man, now!"

Sanjib again said loudly, "What a bunch of fucking amateurs. The answer is no." He then cupped his hands and shouted in various directions, "Come out, come out, wherever you are." No one came out.

The second robber looked at Sanjib's crazy actions and took a swipe with his knife at Sanjib's arm, cutting it slightly and causing it to bleed. Sanjib covered it with a handkerchief. He then said to the three of them, "I'm not kidding; your wallets now, or I'll cut you all," and he waved his knife in Joe's direction. Joe and Sanjib now recognized that this wasn't an FBI practice run, but they still expected the FBI to keep their word on the other part, that they were keeping a close eye on them. With his extensive training, Joe could have quickly disarmed the two robbers but felt it best to make the FBI look good and show their hand. At this point, Joe yelled loudly in all directions, "Okay, you can come out now. We're actually being robbed. Keep your promise."

The robbers couldn't believe what they were seeing from these two guys either and, for a moment, were distracted. Kevin took this split second to pick up a piece of a broken brick and catch the first robber in the head with it. He fell to the ground immediately, bleeding quite a bit. The other robber moved to help him while keeping his blade out toward Joe and Sanjib. Kevin picked several more stones and pieces of brick, giving two to Joe and threatening to use them if the robbers didn't give him his wallet back and leave them alone. Robber number two realized he too could be struck, and his friend killed with another well-placed stone and tossed Kevin's wallet back and led his wounded friend off to the darkness, cursing the three of them in almost a whisper all the way and promising retaliation.

The boys quickly composed themselves and then set about to get Sanjib's flesh wound taken care of.

"Thanks, man. That was quick thinking. You might have saved our lives," said Sanjib to Kevin.

Joe added, "Yeah, thanks, man. That was quick thinking."

"You're welcome," said a still-shaken Kevin. "All of that crazy talk you guys were saying made no sense to them or me. Who the hell were you talking to? When I saw how distracted they were, I grabbed for the first thing I could find. We need to get you to a hospital to get that wound taken care of."

"Let me see it," said Joe and after a quick assessment, "You're lucky, it looks like a shallow flesh wound. Let's buy some antiseptic and bandages and take care of it ourselves." Sanjib nodded.

"What the hell are you talking about?" said a surprised Kevin. "The man has been attacked with a knife!! Let's take him to the hospital and then report it to the police!"

Joe quickly answered back, "No, I don't think that's the best thing to do. If we expose the FBI for screwing things up, they will be pissed off. If they had no intention of helping us, we will have tipped them off that we're wise to their plan. What happens if the attack was a setup, a warning; how do we handle that? I say we keep quiet and go about our normal business but with a little more caution. What happened to us happens all the time to people all over Boston, and the world for that matter. It didn't seem to be anything more than a typical robbery attempt. It's clear, however, that returning here might be dangerous if the two robbers were local."

It was also clear that the FBI had no intent on following through on their guarantee of close surveillance, which had Joe and Sanjib wondering why they had their meeting in the first place.

"What the hell are you talking about? What does the FBI have to do with this? Are we in trouble?" asked a still-troubled Kevin.

Joe had to say something to Kevin to calm him down.

"The FBI told Sanjib and me that because we were back on the project, they would be watching us closely, but obviously they aren't. You aren't involved in this, just me and Sanjib, unless the thugs are on the FBI payroll. We will have to wait and see. For now, however, it is the two of us."

They stopped at a drug store and picked up the appropriate antiseptic ointments and bandages and brought Sanjib home to a deeply upset wife. Kevin left and went home deeply upset as well at what he had wandered into. The next day, Sanjib and Joe had a talk.

"What am I going to do? You saw Mah last night; she was frantic. I'm concerned as well. I have a family to look after and having potential killers after you doesn't help anything or anyone. Mah wants to move anywhere as long as it is far away and safe. That means I need to find a good-paying job, and there are few that pay as well as this."

Joe said, "Let's step back a minute. Neither of the would-be robbers were tiger children, and all they wanted were our wallets. It was a real, random, run-of-the-mill robbery. There's always the possibility of there being more of them, but no one knows if that's the case. I think we need to keep cool about it for a little while longer." Both were concerned Kevin was really shaken up by this and would be leaving soon. The more important message to Joe, however, was that the FBI wasn't watching him closely, substantially increasing his chances of succeeding in his mission to destroy the facility and survive.

UP IN SMOKE

The Pokey facility is in the Lechmere section of East Cambridge. It was originally owned by a colonial-era landowner named Richard Lechmere, a loyalist who fled Boston for England at the beginning of the revolutionary war. The shoreline is shown as Lechmere's Point on Revolutionary war maps, the landing point for British troops enroute to the Battles of Lexington and Concord. The area was developed in the early nineteenth century. Many factories were built in the area, including soap, glass, and furniture. The area also included homes ranging from those for factory workers to superintendents to even factory owners.

As was often the case in many of the early east coast cities, numerous tunnels were dug for a variety of reasons; some were for utility services, while others were officially for movement of products from one building to another but could conveniently be used for avoidance of taxes on finished goods. It wouldn't be the first time a tunnel was built or used to facilitate personal dalliances either.

Joe needed a way to not only severely inhibit the

progress of the Pokey project, but also allow him to personally fall from the face of the earth in the process. His due diligence had paid off. Running adjacent to the Pokey facility and below ground was a large gas line providing services to twenty-two facilities, seven of which were industrial (including CML). There was also a tunnel that had been used for material goods transport. It ran alongside and slightly below the basement of the Pokey building. Abandoned for the last fifty years when the Wollaston Shoe Company shut down, it still appeared at least on maps. It was five feet wide and seven feet tall, through which they would run racks of shoes for further processing from one building to another, hundreds of feet away, and safe from the elements.

Workers would have moved racks of semi-finished shoes to the ironing station where wrinkles in the leather would have been ironed out before proceeding to final inspection and packing. This would have been an integral step of the shoe manufacturing process with every pair of shoes, even if perfect, being inspected. As such, the tunnel would have needed to be maintained to not affect production. Joe had to do a few things:

1. He needed to find a way into the tunnel as far away from the Pokey facility as possible. This he was able to find one hundred and eighty yards away, via a utilities entry for an old MBTA subway station that had been upgraded and replaced ten years earlier. Once inside that room/tunnel, he was able to locate through trial and error, a passage into the

industrial tunnel and follow it to a point alongside the Pokey facility.

All the while, he had to maintain the appearance of abandonment; otherwise, although unlikely, suspicion could arise from a curious transport worker. In the most likely case, he would be viewed as a vagrant looking for a warm place to sleep.

2. He needed to find a way out of the tunnel up through the basement floor of the Pokey building. The basement was used for miscellaneous storage as everything they were using for the project was temperature sensitive and required high security. He placed a small transmitter in an obscure box in a corner of the basement. The transmitter had a lead cover over it so it would only broadcast down. He also put four dead rat bodies around the box as well as some pieces of a sandwich.

Through trial and error, he determined that the transmitter was five feet off to the side of the tunnel wall and four feet up. Luckily, the tunnel was of brick construction, so little by little, he removed the side wall and dig up to the underside of the basement floor. By drilling a few holes, he determined it was six inches of concrete.

. . .

3. He then set out to score an eighteen-inch circle/manhole in the concrete up to the five-and-three-quarter-inch level, the final quarter inch to be cut the day of use.

4. The gas line had a branch running into the basement of the Pokey building. The line had numerous safety shutoff valves in place for emergency or maintenance. Dismantling the safety features and a piece of the three-inch pipe running into the building would be easy and the ensuing explosion of the building and main pipeline would wipe everything out.

All was in place for the last appearance.

FORREST'S THIRD MEETING

Both had agreed to one more meeting before following through on the plan. It was arranged to meet in Boston at the observation deck of the Custom House Tower. The Custom House was built in the 1840s in the same area as Faneuil Hall and Quincy Market. When it was built, it was on the water's edge at the end of the city's docks. This facilitated cargo inspection and levying of duties. In the ensuing century, the harbor was filled in to create more dry land, and the tower is now several hundred yards inland.

The exterior of the tower is Grecian Doric in design and made of granite. From the observation deck on the twenty sixth floor, one could look down on Faneuil Hall and across Boston Harbor.

"Hi, Forrest, how is it going?" asked Joe.

"It's going well. Actually, it's done. Where do we stand from your end?" he asked in return. He was in a serious mood that day.

"We're all set, ninety-eight percent of the way there. There's something else I want to discuss with you though. I'm assuming you and your organization are private citizens and not a part of any government organization."

"As I've told you before, my management is private individuals looking to protect and recoup the wealth that's rightfully theirs."

"Fine, but suppose they are members of a royal family or relatives of a government leader? I could go to jail, and I can't take that risk."

Forrest was now a little agitated, "I don't know what to tell you. You've been officially told we're private investors. What can I say if it turns out differently because I've been lied to as well? What are the courts going to do to you if you were misled?"

"I can't take the risk that I'm being set up to take a fall."

"If we wanted to set you up to do that, we could have already done it with the gold you and your pal brought down from the mountains."

Joe was stunned to hear that, and it showed in his face.

"Yes, we know the two of you found gold on one of the mountains. We don't know what your share was, or what you did with it, but your buddy sold his as soon as he could, and not discreetly, so we could have the both of you locked up for a long time for stealing from the U.S. and other governments. Let's be realistic; it was peanuts in the big scheme of things, chump change.

"You two stole maybe a few million dollars while I'm looking for one trillion dollars. One trillion dollars! Consider it an advance on your commission. Don't forget you have another goal here, and that's to stop this R&D project from finishing and, as you put it, ending the world as we know it. It seems to me we're on the same team." Forrest grew more intense.

"There's another issue I'm powerless to control, and you need to consider. You assume that all you have on the United States side is friends, lots and lots of friends. Get real. If you've pissed anyone off in the past few months by something you did or said, they could have you rubbed out faster than I could. Let's start with the FBI, CIA, NSA, and whomever in Africa that knows you and your pal made the big haul. Someone might put one and one together and come up with 'Joe,' the guy who blew up a hundred-million-dollar secret project and murdered his boss while doing it. Face it—you're a dead man walking."

Joe was silent for a few seconds. Again, Forrest was right. He deeply wanted to kill Pokey. He also put the military, CIA, NSA, and others on the defensive with his revelation in Jizan. It would also be a good idea if he stayed away from poorly lit bars for a while. Surely, someone must be gunning for him.

"Let me be even more direct with you," said Forrest, now leaning forward in his chair. "Very soon, it is possible we may be all that's keeping you alive. Once various parties become aware of your potential knowledge, they too will be gunning for you. You're going to have more enemies than Inspector Clousseau. What if the five hundred acres of land we feel we own in Tokyo, yes, five hundred acres, is currently on the books of one of Japan's oldest companies? Japanese land records go back much further in time than the 1300s. What if we own the land in Shanghai that's now the Bund area and the Pudong Island? What about the Vatican?

"Who knows what mortgages existed seven hundred years ago. What about some of the old European banks? Some of them are in trouble. What if some of their assets belong to my management? What do you think would happen if any of these people found out that an American operative has knowledge that could cost them hundreds of billions of dollars? Hell, I would nuke a city if I thought you were living there to take you out, and deal with the consequences later. Sure, they'll keep us in court for a hundred years, but what's another hundred years when we have already been waiting seven hundred?"

"Okay, you're right. Let's move forward," replied a somber Joe. He decided to take advantage of Forrest's presence and ask him a few open questions.

"Different subject; Help me understand something. I've been surprised recently by finding out that Musa had Jews and Christians in his court. Why?"

"Tell me something I don't know. Musa used Jewish scholars to help set up and teach at the university. They were brilliant, and they were outsiders, which made it easier to monitor them. They were involved then and are still involved now. Do you think it was a coincidence that we met in Paris over a Jewish deli? Regarding Christians, all these guards were and continue to be Christians from East Africa. Once again, they were outsiders from a small sect and beyond internal corruption."

"Now we're getting somewhere. I think your guards hold the key to this puzzle. Why were they selected?"

"I just told you; they are a part of a loyal Christian sect."

"No, there must be more to it. They are physically different. They are all small, young, and look alike. Exactly where are they from? How do you recruit them? Who does the recruiting?"

"I'm not exactly sure, as that's handled by someone else, but I think from Kenya, Ethiopia, Sudan, and from villages at higher locations."

"The FBI says they haven't seen any more of them. Why have they disappeared?"

"What are you talking about? They are still here. There are probably some down the street. They're in every large U.S. city with either a high-tech, military, or large university presence. It's the same in Europe, Africa, and the Middle East where they can more easily blend in with the people. College towns are pretty easy, as are most major capitals." Forrest was impatient at this point. "Are we good to go in one month?"

"Yes, we are. One last question—who do I contact before then if something happens to you?"

After a short pause, Forrest said, "I don't know, and honestly, I don't care."

THE TRAIN TO NEWBURYPORT

For some reason, Joe enjoyed the train. Growing up in upstate New York, he rarely saw a passenger train, let alone ride on one. Nara, on the other hand, had too many memories of over-crowded and aromatic trains in her native Sudan with no air conditioning in that oppressive climate. She was a good sport, however, and joined Joe for the ride from Boston to Newburyport for what should be a fun weekend.

Little by little, she relaxed and became more comfortable with who she was and with Joe. She even wore blue jeans, running shoes, and a baseball cap on the train, something that never would have happened in prior years. Some habits are hard to break, however, and dress for that evening's dinner would revert to form.

Newburyport had been a trading port dating from revolutionary times, having been repurposed in recent years to a very up and coming, upscale entertainment/weekends/livable city. Many of the buildings pre-dated the Revolutionary War and reflected the immense wealth of one of the British colonies' busiest seaports.

He got them a room in a two-hundred-year-old hotel from which they could walk to shops, the waterfront, restaurants, and the beach. He and Nara were still studying each other carefully. They hadn't been seeing each other all that long, but as one gets older, one tended to speed up the process and size people up faster. Joe's insecurities with women were understandable given all that he had been through. Nara was a quiet soul, perhaps because of her upbringing, or perhaps because of her suffering. She wasn't as outgoing as Lexi had been, but then again, Lexi was younger and a curvaceous blonde that everyone took a second look at, and she knew it. Nara was six years older than Lexi and Indian. The second looks she would get would be people wondering if she were black or Latina. She too was sweet in nature, but a serious, calm sweet. She created none of the anxieties in Joe that Lexi did. He trusted her completely. In any case, Joe had fallen in love, again.

Nara looked at Joe and wondered what kind of a man she was getting involved with. A man whose life was "classified" by the American government from the age of twenty-two onward. She knew he too had been scarred by the loss of a loved one but, like her, he kept that pain well-hidden and controlled. He enjoyed life and was an attractive man. Perhaps it was the mystery, but she too had fallen in love, again.

The first afternoon was spent walking the streets, observing the beautiful homes that had been built centuries earlier by the prosperous merchant class and enjoying leisurely cups of coffee in the many sidewalk cafes. The evening was for dinner, dancing, and making love.

The second day began with a leisurely breakfast in the hotel's period dining area. The balance of the day was spent in the many antique and secondhand shops, as well as the many unique stores in the downtown area. The end of the day approached while they walked the sands of Plum Island. They stopped for a minute and sat in the approach to a sand dune and took a little time to look out over the breaking waves, the lighthouses, and the beautiful summer homes along the shore. It was getting a little chilly, and Nara moved up between Joe's knees so he could provide some warmth by wrapping his arms around her. The scene was serene. Joe nuzzled close to her neck and whispered in her ear, "I love you."

"I know."

"What do you mean 'I know?'"

"Just that," cooed Nara. "Actions speak louder than words. A woman knows these kinds of things, especially a mature woman." Now her tone turned serious. "What I don't know is where do we go from here? We're still young enough to get married and raise a family, but I'm not sure who you are and what you do and what you want from life? I have this uneasy feeling that you're in a lull, you know like the lull between storms. You're unpredictable. Some women thrive on that insecure feeling, but not me. It's not that I don't trust you, honey, but I worry about the karma you've surrounded yourself with. I really want the husband and the house with a white picket fence."

Joe whispered back, "I understand and believe me when I say I have a similar goal. After this project is over, I see me moving on to something entirely different, like herding goats or growing corn. Maybe becoming a schoolteacher and being home every night."

Nara replied with a slight smile, "I hope so, and by the way, I love you too." A kiss and a caress held them there until it was nearly dark. They returned to the city for a pleasant meal at one of the many seafood restaurants. After that, it was a forty-five-minute ride by train back to Boston, and home.

FOURTEEN

The Last Staff Meeting

It was a miserable, dark, rainy day in June, and the streets showed it. In the old sections of some New England cities, one could still find cobblestone streets that were laid down over two hundred years ago, long before asphalt became available. This section of Cambridge was one of those cases. While much of the street had been paved over during the past century, the sides near the curbstones and gutters showed their age with exposed and slippery cobblestones in abundance. It was something you lived with. You dealt with it with raincoats, umbrellas, and boots.

Skip waited for a few stragglers to hang up their gear and enter the room before beginning his monthly staff meeting.

"Good morning, people. I have a busy day so let's get going. Mildred, you go first."

"We're struggling to fill the last remaining open positions. Competition for good candidates is strong. The economy around here is on fire. Making matters worse is the tightening action the government has made regarding security clearances. They made two changes just last week. The available pool of competent workers is small, and I think the solution will have to be sweetening the offers to make working here more attractive."

Sanjib and Kevin wasted no time in jumping in.

"If you're going to 'sweeten' offers to new employees, you had better start taking a close look at your existing employees. If they don't jump ship before we're fully staffed, they will certainly leave after hearing what new hires are getting. People can't keep their mouths shut when it comes to what they're earning," said Kevin.

"Mildred, how much sweetening are you talking about?" asked Skip.

"Possibly ten percent."

"Then you had better consider ten to fifteen percent for your existing staff, or it's adios, amigos," added Sanjib.

"Sanjib, is that Hindi for see you later?" shot back Kevin.

Sanjib, acting surprised, said, "Why yes and, hey, when did you learn Hindi?" The crosstalk in the meeting took over, and Skip was forced to raise his voice to bring things back under control.

"Let's keep it down to a roar, huh, people? I don't know what's possible, but we have to find a way to meet our commitment. Bob, where do we stand on our budget vs. actual expenses?"

"Year to date, we're five percent under budget solely due to not being able to completely staff up. Remember that your admin people will need the same increases, or they too will be out the door."

"Before I go up the ladder looking for more money, please give me your best shot on where we will be at the end of the fiscal year, assuming we can't find anyone else with the salaries offered and we spread that money among our existing employees. Also, do some checking with your financial and (turning to Mildred) human resource peers on how they're handling this crunch. The rest of you, give me an honest assessment of how far behind schedule we will be without the extra people. Next, Sanjib?"

"We're making good progress despite being short one person. Computer speeds keep ramping up, and we can keep pace with Kevin's team. Decision-making abilities keep improving. Over to you, Kevin."

"We're moving right along on target. The previously reported issues on the displays still exist. Our hardware is keeping pace with their software."

"Thank you. Joe?"

"I'm moving ahead like the others. I'm working with the NSA group on several related sensor and drone issues. That's it."

"Okay, folks, thanks for coming," said Skip. "Those of you with assignments, please have the results back to me in exactly one week so I can put things in motion and, hopefully, have something to report back to you at our next meeting. Good day."

With that, Kevin, Sanjib, and Joe went back to their offices for one hour, after which they all went out to grab a sandwich for lunch. It was obvious to Joe that something was on Kevin's mind.

"What's up, Kevin? You have a distant look on your face. Did you have a bad night?"

Sanjib added, "Yah, Joe's right. Are you having girl problems? Guy problems? Is it something I can explain to you?"

Kevin shrugged a little bit and said, "It's not women or guys, and (looking at Sanjib) you would be among the last people I would approach. I'm just sitting here after another dumb meeting. On top of that, I could be arrested for assault with a deadly weapon, a rock, or worse, robbed again or even killed by either robbers or some mystery group, all because I'm working on a project with you two guys. Heck, the project itself might not make it. Yup, not a good place to be, wouldn't you say?"

Joe said, "I don't think anyone wants to hurt or kill you. You just happened to be with us that night. I can't imagine there are people out there looking for you."

Kevin shot back, "How does my position differ from Sanjib's? He just saved your life, that's all, just like I did the other night. I know nothing, and he might know nothing, or less, but will that save our necks? I don't know about you, Sanjib, but hanging around here or even each other at this point might not be good for our health. I have a girlfriend now, a nice girl. She isn't going to be happy to find out about this or get involved with it, or me."

It was clearer than ever that Kevin would be seeking greener and safer pastures soon.

<u>Goodbye</u>

Joe realized he too needed to consider the next step, given that a lot of people were likely gunning for him. He had already discussed this with Forrest, but now needed to do the same with Sanjib and separately with Nara. He realized there was a risk in talking openly with each of them, but Sanjib had risked his life to save Joe's, and Nara was his love. The opportunity with Sanjib arose after they had finished lunch one day. It was a nice June afternoon, and Joe suggested they walk to a mini park where they sat on a bench to talk.

"I've been thinking a lot about the robbery incident and your being slashed and the safety of your family. What you do as a result is obviously your business. I thought I should give you a head's up on where my head is at. It's eighty percent me that whoever is behind this is after. I'm the one they need to take out. You're twenty percent of the picture. You were in the wrong place at the wrong time."

"That's not to say they won't take you out too, but their number-one priority is me. Sometime soon, maybe very soon, we'll see, I may disappear in an apparent violent fashion. I'll make every attempt to survive, but there will be no guarantees. I'm telling you this because it may involve Nara. We have become very close, and I'm not sure how she will react to such a dramatic change in living, but it's obvious to me that I'm a dead man if I stay around here much longer.

"When it happens, with or without Nara, assume we're dead and react accordingly. Too much of a reaction and the powers that be might be suspicious. Too little and they might be suspicious. If we or I'm still alive, you'll be contacted at an appropriate time. If you're not contacted in time, she or we're indeed dead."

"Why are you telling me this?"

"Because my decision might affect your decision, and because you and your family are all that Nara has for family in America. It's going to be very hard on her to just walk away forever."

"She is a nice girl, take good care of her," implored a serious Sanjib.

"I will."

Sanjib had become a little reflective at this point, "Whatever happens, we should agree right now to contact each other in two years' time."

"That's a good idea. No communication at all about our meeting prior to the meeting itself; we just do it. Now the question is, where?"

"It's obvious, three p.m., same date, Faneuil Hall."

"Obvious," They gave each other a hug and went back to work.

Later that day, Joe had to make one of the most difficult and serious presentations of his life. He and Nara had been dating very seriously. They had begun discussions about moving in with each other and making it a more permanent relationship. Joe was quite serious at dinner in her home, and Nara noticed it. "You aren't yourself tonight. What's bothering you?"

"We need to talk," said a somber and slightly shaking

Joe. He asked her to join him on the living room sofa. "I've enjoyed being with you and…"

She cut him off, placing her forefinger on his mouth and said in an excited voice, "You're breaking up with me? Is that what you're trying to say? You're breaking up with me?"

"No, no, just the opposite," comforted Joe. "I want to make it permanent, forever. It's the circumstances of living with me that have me in this serious mood. The people who tried to kill me at Faneuil Hall are still around. They tried to kill me in Africa too, because of project Pokey. I need to get out of this line of work and disappear, at least from the Northeast."

"Oh, you mean like the witness protection program?"

"Not quite. The government agencies are part of the problem. I need to fall off the face of the earth without their help. Fake my own death."

"How are you going to do that?" questioned Nara, now a bit calmer.

"The paperwork like fake birth certificates, passports, driver's licenses, and social security numbers are easy, and very quick to get. The issue is appearing to die in a horrific, untraceable accident and starting life all over again, in some other part of the USA or even out of the country."

"Joe, I love you. What is it you're trying to tell me?" said Nara in a soft and soothing voice.

With this, Joe bent down on one knee.

"I want you to marry me and together fall off the face of the earth. It must appear that we died beyond recognition in a horrific accident. We will disappear from Boston and surface somewhere else in America as different people doing different things. We can tell no one, give no advance warning, or leave any clues. I have no choice, but you do. I know you have friends and family here and a great job. If you say no, I'll understand. If you say yes, we need to leave soon with only the clothes on our back, our wallet and pocketbook. I've already set aside enough money for us to live on for quite a while if need be. We'll be okay."

After a hard swallow, a nervous Joe popped the question the best he could;

"I love you very much, Nara, and want to raise a family and spend the rest of my life with you. Under these circumstances, will you marry me?"

She looked deep into his eyes. "I can always get another job," said Nara, ever so relaxed and stroking Joe's hair, "I have only Sanjib's family to call my own. As much as I love them dearly, you're lucky if you get two chances at love during your life, so the answer is yes."

They fell into a long and serious kiss and embrace, sharing and exchanging tears of joy, and spent the night in each other's arms. The following morning, Joe put the plan into motion; the big day was coming.

THE LAST APPEARANCE

The Fourth of July is a big deal in Massachusetts, particularly in greater Boston. This is where it all began, starting with the Boston Massacre to The Boston Tea Party to Paul Revere's ride, and it goes on. The highlight in Boston was the annual concert given that evening by the Boston Pops Orchestra in the Hatch Shell along the Charles River Esplanade. It was performed before a live audience that often topped five hundred thousand people, followed by a spectacular fireworks display shot off from barges in the Charles River. There would usually be one to two million people watching the activities live on both sides of the river and many millions more on television.

This extravaganza required the services of thousands of police and fire personnel to guarantee the safety of the crowd as well as the homes, buildings, boats, and schools in the immediate vicinity. All eyes were on the fireworks. At the last minute on July third, Joe told Skip that he would be in the office for a few hours the next day to finish up something that was overdue. He thought of asking permission to use the roof as a vantage point but deemed it risky as Skip could have said no, or he could have invited everyone to use it.

That morning, Joe and Nara prepared for the event. They filled a duffel bag with spare clothes to change into and grooming equipment. Joe had already set up separate bank and credit card accounts under assumed names and left their existing bank accounts nearly unchanged to avoid suspicion. He had even deposited a few small checks the day before to further mask his intentions. New driver's licenses and social security numbers had been issued as well.

At three p.m., they left her home for the last time and drove to the Pokey facility in Joe's Ford Bronco, carrying lounge chairs and a cooler with them. They were making it obvious that they were there to make use of the rooftop viewing area. Nara set up their chairs and arranged a few props on the roof. Joe finished cutting through the basement floor and other necessary preparations. He shut off the main gas valve and removed a piece of pipe after it, which would expose the full flow to the basement once reopened. He also disabled all the safety valves ahead of the main valve. All systems were now a go.

While on the roof at eight thirty p.m. and the night just starting to get dark, they took selfies of themselves in their chairs, smiling and drinking beer and wine, and then sent them to a few friends, Sanjib and Mah via social media. Immediately after, they made their way down to the first floor to put the rest of the plan in motion.

The first thing was to change their appearance. For this, they ducked into the men's room. Joe shaved off his light beard and moustache and gave himself a quick haircut, the full extent of which would be covered by a generic baseball cap. Nara let Joe trim her hair just enough to make a difference and hid his handiwork under a baseball cap. They both changed from running shoes, shorts, and short-sleeve shirts to shoes and socks, slacks and long-sleeve shirts. Having finished, they left the men's room and made a beeline to the stairs leading to the roof to gather their remaining things.

"Hi guys!" shouted Skip from the top of the stairs. While they had been changing, Skip for some reason had come to the office at a very odd time. "I figured you might stay to see the fireworks and figuring it was a pretty good spot to see them, I thought I would join you." Joe and Nara were at first visibly rattled but self-corrected quickly.

"Skip, you scared the bejeepers out of me!" said Nara. "Couldn't you've said hello before climbing the stairs? Did you bring your kids?"

"I'm sorry, Nara, that wasn't very nice of me. I came alone. The kids are either at their mother's or the beach. It's just me."

"Well, welcome and have a beer or would you prefer a glass of white wine?" Joe smiled.

"A beer will do fine, thank you. Say what happened to your beard? Nara, your hair looks shorter, too. And what's with the long clothes?"

"I insisted on long sleeves and pants against the mosquitos," was Nara's fast and pragmatic reply.

"And the beard was beginning to itch, so I shaved it off this morning. Same with the hair, it was too long for the summer,"

These questions were too pointed and obvious. Skip must have seen the social media photos, but how? He wasn't on either Nara or Joe's network. Someone in their networks must have forwarded them to Skip, or Forrest had hacked into them and done the same. If he had seen the photos, he would have known that his shave and their haircuts had happened in the past thirty minutes and that something was up. If Forrest had tipped him off, he knew exactly what was going on. Was it a big enough deal for him to drive all the way in to work to do what, watch the fireworks with them? That was highly unlikely. He must have seen the photos, or he would have called Joe to confirm if they were there.

He was there to observe what they were doing and to

take the appropriate action. Either option didn't look good for Nara and Joe. Someone had tipped Skip off. How many people was he spying for? Joe had to make a fast decision on whether to take Skip's life before or during the explosion or postpone the activity. There wouldn't be another chance like this to cover things, and Skip was a spy or double spy, likely to take action tomorrow or kill them that night. It was an easy "survival of the fittest" decision. Skip must die.

The next forty-five minutes were all chitchat. At nine thirty p.m., it was completely dark when Nara received a call on her cell phone from Mah. She started to speak quite emotionally and loudly in Hindi into the phone and went down the stairs for more privacy. Apparently, Mah had received a text message from Nara in Hindi saying only, 'Goodbye. I love you,' and wanted to know what that was all about. Joe just looked at Skip, shrugged his shoulders, and opened another beer. At 9:35 p.m., she hung up with Mah and immediately received a text message from Mah. At 9:40 p.m., Nara hadn't returned yet.

Joe looked at his watch and said to Skip, "The fireworks start in five minutes. I'm going to take a pee and find Nara so that she is up here in time," Skip nodded, beer in hand, and kept looking skyward and off went Joe ostensibly to accomplish those tasks leaving Skip on the roof.

He found Nara waiting by the door leading to the basement with her hands behind her and looking nervous and upset. Before Joe could say much more than what's wrong, Skip appeared suddenly, having followed Joe down from the roof and loudly said, "What's going on here? Why aren't you up on the roof watching the fireworks?" Joe and Nara had a guilty look on their faces. "What are you two hiding?" No answer from either.

Skip turned and slowly walked away to do who knows what. Perhaps go up and watch the fireworks or report Joe and Nara to the police. Maybe even get a gun to kill them. Nara couldn't take the chance of being exposed and jailed at what was one of the most important times of her life. To Joe's surprise and horror, she brought her hands forward and with a revolver in hand, took two quick steps towards Skip, and with eyes closed, frantically pulled the trigger and prayed there were bullets in the chambers. From five feet away, she fired them all, hitting Skip three times in the back, one bullet piercing his heart and killing him instantly.

As she stood there shaking, she dropped the gun and passed her cell phone to Joe to show him the text message received from Mah just a few minutes earlier that said, "There's a gun in the top right-hand drawer." She had correctly assumed it was Joe's desk and quickly retrieved it "just in case." They couldn't stop to discuss the who/what/where of this situation; they had to get the hell out of there quickly.

Joe opened the basement door, and they both scurried down. He lowered Nara into the tunnel, gave her a flashlight, and told her to run as fast as she could to the right at least two hundred feet away. He took her cell phone from her and made sure it was off. He did the same with his own just to be sure there would be no premature explosion. He put both and the gun on the floor near the gas valve. From the loud booms, Joe knew the fireworks had started. He then opened the valve and let it fill the room with gas.

As on the mountain, he left two cell phones with obscure telephone numbers and a failsafe sparker to ignite the gas on his signal. He lowered himself into the tunnel, pulling a steel plate he had cut over the hole to hopefully withstand the pressure and heat of a premature explosion and give them a little more of a safety margin in escaping. Flashlight in hand, he ran as fast as he could toward Nara.

They emerged from the tunnel with a half-filled bottle of wine as a prop, leaving the flashlights behind, and headed to the subway station at the Science Museum. From there, they caught a subway to South Station and then a train to New York City. Precious time was ticking. Joe had originally wanted to wait at least an hour before detonation, but with Skip dead on the first floor and not knowing if more people might show up unannounced at the office, he had to act much quicker.

As soon as they arrived at South Station, bought their tickets, and boarded the train, Joe made the calls from a stolen cell phone. The ensuing explosion was far louder than the fireworks finale, which was ongoing. By the time the Cambridge fire department could muster a sufficient squad to the scene, there was nothing left but ashes, glassified brick, and a deep hole in the ground.

On the train ride to New York City, they avoided talking about any of this, limiting chitchat to how nice it will be to see various aunts and uncles again. Inside, Joe wondered who set up Skip and who sent the text messages from what appeared to be Mah's address. Who owned the gun and had it placed in Joe's desk? It wasn't a gun of Joe's, as it was a revolver. He had moved on a long time ago to the more sophisticated and difficult to use semi-automatic pistols. Someone had placed a gun there that the widest group of people could use. It didn't take much time to arrive at a plausible person—his Asian friend. It was clever too. There was now one less person in the loop, one less witness to what had been going on, and one less potential leak.

TOMORROW

The explosion and subsequent fireball were the number one story on the television news, the internet, social media, and in the newspapers the next day. The video shots of the fireball were dramatic. It caused the evacuation of buildings within three hundred feet of the former building. The damage to other properties in the immediate area was well into the tens of millions of dollars. Screaming headlines in the Boston and New York City tabloids pronounced a "Fourth Fireball Finale" at a government research building that overshadowed the evening's earlier display.

They were lucky their train took off on time. As a precautionary measure, subsequent train departures and arrivals were delayed.

Officially, the explosion was attributed to a pipeline valve leak at a utility facility conducting research on how to slow global warming. It wasn't until the following day when neither Joe, Skip, or Nara showed up for work or could be found that it started to sink in with the schools, social media, and the project people that they were missing. Sanjib came forward with the selfie that Nara had sent him just before the fireworks began.

The situation presented the FBI and project people with a public relations disaster. Several people related to the Faneuil Hall shootings and the project were in the building when the explosion occurred. On top of that, the wife of a man run down and killed in a hit and run accident in Somerville and a Harvard employee was also among the missing/incinerated. All coincidental. No matter what anyone would tell you, the perception was that of a professional hit, but by whom, and why?

A problem they had to deal with was the burnt remains of Joe's Bronco and Skip's Nissan that had been in the parking lot. Although there wasn't much left of them, they were registered to real specific people. The government had to admit they were in the building at the time of the explosion, taking advantage of the rooftop to gain a good vantage point for the evening's fireworks display. Nara's final selfie took care of that detail.

In the meantime, the worm that had been placed in the software a few months before had already taken effect and severely damaged the integrity of the results. The torching of all the hardware and the program manager was enough to place the program on the back burner for "officially" many months, but realistically for several years minimum. The program was still valuable to the government as the platform for several secret applications so it would be revived. The official reason was to rebuild and restart, but the unofficial reasons were to find out who ordered the hit and why, and to dig into whatever projects the other parties had going on as a result of whatever they could steal from Pokey. The employees were valuable too and would need a new home to work from, a new boss to work for, and an incentive not to jump ship and move to a more stable work environment.

Joe now wondered if there was a second mole at Pokey working for Forrest. Having Skip place a gun in Joe's desk that could be used against him was a little bit of a risk.

At this point, the former Joe and Nara were on a train enroute to Miami for the next chapter in their lives as Mitchell Santiago and his Nicaraguan wife Gisele.

SUNSET

It was a lonely, ominous wind blowing that day. In years past, Joe might have noticed it, but things had changed. It was fall again, and Joe and Nara had a lot to think about now with her pregnant. Marriage had occurred several months earlier, using assumed names, places of birth, etc. Among the questions circulating in their heads were, where would they live? The problem with Massachusetts and the Northeast in general was that there would always be the pull of academia and spies!

Other than where to live long term, they had their future well planned out. Nara would be a stay-at-home mother, and Joe would find a job that didn't require a resume or references as his entire adult life had been in the shadowy world of international espionage. Fortunately, the discreet sale of his gold bar had given them enough money to live on for several years. He could cover for a while as a "consultant."

He did give some thought to returning to Africa to recover more of the gold on top of Mount Stanley but quickly gave that up as being exceedingly risky, if not impossible. Previously, he had the support of dozens of armed guards and porters, and military support facilities and airplanes through which he could move restriction free. Quietly selling one million dollars in gold was dramatically safer and easier than one hundred million or one billion dollars' worth. Better safe than sorry or more likely, dead. That didn't stop him from wondering, however, how much gold was up there and on other mountains!

They chose to move to Miami where the weather was pleasant most of the year, the culture intriguing, and few questions were asked of people. They leased an ocean view condominium to live in with space for Joe to run his business, whatever that became.

Joe knew that running away from a previous life and starting over completely new was far more difficult than people could imagine. To start, everything he used to do was off limits. He could no longer work in the same industries or work with the same people. That would expose him. He needed to change his looks. He couldn't patronize the same organizations anymore, be they airlines, hotel chains, or restaurants as he might be recognized.

The same was even true with merchants he purchased things from, especially over the internet. His purchasing patterns for things he bought for himself and others would be recognized and tracked. (The same was true for any technical websites he might visit. If the government had any suspicion Joe was still alive, they might offer up "Pokey bait" to lure him and track him down). If he were going to do it, it was best if he could get lost in a large metropolis, far away from home, and changing as much about himself as possible.

In any case, life was good, the weather warmer, and the new Mitch and Gisele were enjoying a Sunday afternoon football game on television at their favorite local pub, The Southern Charm. The game was exciting, and the crowd really into it. At one point in the fourth quarter after a touchdown was scored, a bearded man wearing glasses and a Miami Dolphins cap leaned over from the next table and said, "Hey Joe, you think the Patriots will make it to the championship this year?"

Acknowledgments

Many people contributed to the making of this novel. My wife Phyllis and son Andrew were among the earliest supporters. The guidance of accomplished writer Julien Ayotte was very instrumental. Friends Mary Lou Anderson and Steve Laham lent their expertise in editing the content. Jennifer Givner created the outstanding book covers and maps, and Jennipher Tripp skillfully formatted its contents.

My greatest thanks go to my longtime friend Bill Jones, who provided support and encouragement from start to finish.

Thank you all.

64826984R10157

Made in the USA
Middletown, DE
30 August 2019